THE VOGUE

Eoin McNamee's novels include *Resurrection Man*, which was longlisted for the Booker Prize and later made into a film, *The Blue Tango*; *Orchid Blue*, described by John Burnside in the *Guardian* as 'not only a political novel of the highest order but also that rare phenomenon, a genuinely tragic work of art'; and *Blue is the Night*, which won the 2015 Kerry Group Irish Novel of the Year Award. He lives in Sligo.

by the same author

THE LAST OF DEEDS
LOVE IN HISTORY
RESURRECTION MAN
THE BLUE TANGO
ORCHID BLUE
BLUE IS THE NIGHT
THE ULTRAS
12.23

THE VOGUE

EOIN McNAMEE

FABER & FABER

First published in 2018
by Faber & Faber Ltd
Bloomsbury House
74–77 Great Russell Street
London WC1B 3DA

Typeset by Faber & Faber Ltd
Printed and bound by CPI Group (UK) Ltd, Croydon CR0 4YY

A CIP record for this book
is available from the British Library

ISBN 978–0–571–33160–4

FSC
www.fsc.org
MIX
Paper from
responsible sources
FSC® C020471

2 4 6 8 10 9 7 5 3 1

For Dermot Healy
His chapel of salt

Pirnmill Aerodrome, Morne
16th November 2000

The sandpit had been opened. A yellow excavator stood by the side of the pit, its bucket raised. Swags of unfurled bandage hung from the bucket tangs, filthy and dripping. An articulated Scania with a covered trailer was backed up to the broken ground at the edge, its hydraulic rams half-extended. A fluorescent works light hung on jack chain from a corroded derrick. Three men rendered into silhouettes stood between the pit and the light. They stood without moving, their heads bent towards the opening at their feet, functionaries to the merciless night.

The bottom of the pit was half-filled with water. Syringes. Wound dressings rank with old blood and human tissue. Rusted scalpel blades and theatre gowns bundled and discarded. Used drug vials and transfusion sacs floated in the water. A woman's skeletal remains clad in vile rags lay halfway up the pit wall as though she had crawled from it, matter adhering to her hair and clothes. As though she had looked for mercy and found there none. Across the sandy fen to the north of the darkened aerodrome, chapel bells rang for the ascension.

One

The Negro sits without moving. In the execution shed the apparatus is being made ready. The hood. The rope. The pinnings. Coir matting has been placed on the floor and against the walls to deaden sound but the prisoners can hear the hammering and tool work.

In his autobiography the hangman Albert Pierrepoint stated his dislike for the American hanging method. Pierrepoint liked to have his prisoner sitting with his back to the door so that he could be taken by surprise and pinioned. Pierrepoint said he could get the prisoner from the cell to the drop in ninety seconds. He prided himself on it. The Americans insisted that the prisoner wear full dress uniform with all marks of rank and insignia removed. The charges and sentence must be read to the condemned man at the foot of the scaffold. The Americans wanted the execution to be procedural, ornate. The prisoner must be reminded of his guilt. The executioners must be reminded of their duty. They imagine the antechamber of death to be a place of drama, laconic asides, last-minute admissions.

'Pierrepoint won't sneak up on me,' Martinez said, 'I'm going out the American way.'

Martinez had been sentenced to death for the murder of a military policeman.

'Kind of justice I like,' Martinez said. 'Court martial took a day. No appeal. Straight and to the point. I got no complaints. The bastard MP had it coming.'

Martinez said he was going to stand facing the door of the death cell so that Pierrepoint could not take him by surprise.

'Full dress kit. I'll be standing to attention. Walk out of there like a man.'

Shepton Mallet has been under United States military jurisdiction since 1942. The men call to each other softly from the windows. They are not normally permitted to communicate but on the eve of an execution the guards are lenient.

'Hooper,' Davis said, 'you there?'

'I'm here.'

'I seen Pierrepoint go into the governor's house when they brought me down.'

'What'd he look like?'

'Ordinary man. Owns a bar in Oldham. He hanged one of his own customers, gentleman by the name of Corbitt. Corbitt killed his girlfriend and wrote "whore" on her forehead.'

'Man deserved to hang then.'

'Bar was called Help the Poor Struggler.'

'Strange name for a bar.'

'Strange thing for a hangman to end up behind a long counter.'

Hooper had been shackled to Davis in the back of the utility truck that brought them to the prison. Davis was from Chicago, a thin, talkative man. He said he was double-jointed. He could

4

slip his hands out of the cuffs any time he wanted, he said. All you had to do was give the word. They passed through Bristol at the dead of night, the town under blackout. Driving through the Mendip Hills. Stubble fields, gold and red as though the moonlight burned them. Passing through the towns of Clifton and Winterbourne. Passing through Evercreech and Frome.

'Where you from, son?' Davis said.

'East Atlanta. Key Road.'

'Your first time out of the States?'

'First time out of Atlanta, Georgia.'

Davis spat over the tailgate of the truck.

'And dearly you wish you had never left it.'

'You got that right.'

'What you doing there?' Hooper had turned away from Davis and brought his shackled hands together on the bench. He was working on the varnish with the edge of the shackle.

'Writing my name.'

'You won't half cop it if the redcaps find what you done.'

'I'm just doing the initial. That's as far as I'm going.'

'As far as you're going is Shepton Mallet. Last stop on the line.'

The Negro asked where they were and the MP escort said they were close to Glastonbury. Davis told him about Glastonbury Tor. He said that ley lines ran under the front gate of Shepton Mallet.

'What are ley lines?

'Ley lines is the lines of power. The ancient people knew them.'

'Boy is all caught up by the ancient stuff,' the MP said, 'caught up by it till he's caught up by the neck hisself.'

'Reckon the Negro here believes in that voodoo stuff?' Davis said.

'Voodoo is from Haiti,' Hooper said.

'Same difference. Nothing godly in any of it.'

Hooper says nothing. His grandma told him there are demons out there. She'd seen it herself. Souls are devoured.

If he stood on his bed Hooper could see the execution shed. The shed was a windowless red-brick two-storey extension attached to the limestone wall of the old prison. An internal door opened from the main body of the prison into the execution chamber. The trapdoor opened onto a downstairs room with an external door. The external door faced the steel door of the morgue in the next building. January frost on the ground at first light. Fifty minutes after dawn the ground-floor door opened. Two men carried Martinez's body on a stretcher like something they had stolen. He could hear the sound of their boots on the loose clinker on the ground as though they struck iron there. His grandmother had told stories of graves opened by night and bodies thieved. She said the darkness called out to its own.

Hooper turned away from the window and lay down on his bed. He closed his eyes. He had left East Atlanta eight months earlier in order to enlist. He had come into New York by bus through the Jersey turnpike. The suburban city lost in dusk, snow flurries blowing through the grid of clapboard houses. America looking lost in a wintry dream of itself. He could see the towers of Manhattan in the distance but he was more aware of the cracked road surface, rubbish piled in the freeway margins, caught in broken chain-link fences.

He had expected more. A city that was striven for, epic, rising out of the historic swamplands. Passing road signs. Newark. Idlewild. The lost townships. He wanted to see skyscrapers close up, those theatres of the air.

He stayed in a Negro hotel on the margins of the wholesale district. His grandma had given him a silver half-dollar when he left home. The coin had a picture of Liberty dressed as a Roman goddess on one side and an eagle on the other. Liberty was carrying branches and an American flag over her shoulder. His grandma had raised him and knew all there was to know.

Hooper lifted the side of the wardrobe and hid the half-dollar underneath then went out into the city. There were braziers burning on the street. The night was loud with stoop-talk, Negro gutturals. The streets smelt of rotting fruit. Crates of vegetables piled high on the sidewalk. He looked into warehouses and stores, the massive girdered interiors, feeling that he was getting a grasp on the inner matter of the city, the iron-joisted substance of it. It was cold and he saw steam rising from the sidewalk grilles. It surprised him again that the city was gritty, earthbound. On a street corner a prostitute offered him sexual favours.

She walked in front of him down a lightless alleyway between two buildings, the metal fire escapes over his head, the woman small, light-boned, a scampering figure of folklore mischief, Hooper knowing he was being led out of the light.

She called to him from the doorway of a building annexe, a windowless boiler room, the entrance a dark opening, the door off its hinges. Ivy grew down from the roof. He knows she'll be waiting for him in the dark, a princess, her skin flawless, the lips red. Something from a story where fingers were pricked by spindles, poisoned apples.

He'd felt this in rooms before. The place in Decatur. The place in Little Five Points. The smeared walls, the smell of urine. Here the wall covered in vile scrawls. There are bottles on the floor, torn clothing. A chaise longue with horsehair stuffing protruding. He felt his way to the settee and sat down.

The woman stands over him. His hair is matted with sweat. There is dried spittle in the corner of his mouth. Her mouth is pursed in distaste. A book lay on the floor and he lifted it. Horseman of the King. The Story of John Wesley.

'Is this yours?'

'Does it look like mine?'

She lay down on a wool blanket. She was a carnal leftover, the rouged leavings of the night.

Two

Pirnmill Aerodrome
20th November 2000

Early morning. Grey skies. You could see a long way across
the aerodrome to the sign for Ocean Sands caravan park.
Looking across the block plant. The remnants of some spent
industry. Overworked resources, seeping pollutants exhausted.
Machinery dented and rusted. A dumper truck with flat tyres.
Machine parts leaked diesel sludge onto the concrete apron.
You started to wonder what had led to this abandonment.
What catastrophe had come to pass.

Cole imagined the malign traffic that had flowed through
this yard. Customs, police, tax inspectors. The administrative
weather set at steady rain. Cole looked in the largest shed. A
door creaked somewhere at the back, the noise amplified in
the girdered ceiling. The place reeked of secret histories, illicit
commerce.

He got out of the car. An elderly man in a white shirt with
bloodspots on the collar was waiting for him beside the Ocean
Sands sign. He looked like a lone survivalist, edgy, spooked.
He kept looking past Cole. As if he knew what was out there.
As if he knew it would come again.

'You're Mr Upritchard?'

'Reverend Wesley Upritchard.'

'You're the registered owner of this part of aerodrome land, including the caravan park.'

'I own the caravan park but I don't know you.'

'John Cole, representing the Ministry of Defence interest in this matter.'

'There was never any luck in this land,' Wesley Upritchard said. 'Anything said as to her identity?'

'No.'

'Nor any word how long she's been in the ground?'

'No.'

'The sand will hold you down there until it's good and ready to let you go.'

'How long has the illegal dumping been going on?'

'I don't know. Lorries come in off the ferry and go out again the same way. Nobody knows nothing about them.'

'They had to cross your land to get to the pit.'

'I cannot witness to that nor deny it. I have seen lights here at night and thought it Ministry of Defence people.'

'Have you told that to the police?'

'I have spoken to Sergeant Lynch.'

'Have you made a formal statement?'

'We're of the one mind on it, nothing further to add.'

'Everyone has something to add.'

'And what do you have?'

'I have the right to inspect all documentation in relation to the freehold, leasehold, transfers and otherwise.'

'You think one of your own was responsible for what happened to her? A soldier? Is that why you're here?'

'We don't know what happened to her.'

'The sands not like right ground.'

'What do you mean?'

'The sands shift. Things travel down there. Because she was found here doesn't mean she was put in the ground here.'

Cole looked out over the tailings pond beside the block yard. A crust of dried sand on top and underneath the liquid tonnage. Deep tectonic movement. The land shifting beneath your feet.

'She should have stayed down there.'

'I don't think she had a choice in the matter.'

'She should have stayed down there until she was called.'

'Called?'

'On the day of Resurrection.'

'Do you have land maps here, Reverend Upritchard, deeds, anything like that?'

'No.'

'I can just look them up in the land registry. As I said, I have jurisdiction in this.'

'There is only one jurisdiction we are answerable to.'

'I need to find Sergeant Lynch.'

'Try the Legion at the harbour. It's the kind of place you might find a sporting man.'

There was racing on the television with the sound turned down, jockeys in muted silk turning into the home straight. Kempton Park, Chepstow. Labouring towards the line in rain-blown provincial racetracks. Sleet coming in from the sea against the Legion windows. The girl behind the bar was Latvian, the product of some gritty Baltic seaport. Her small dissatisfied-looking mouth turned down at the corners.

'I was told Sergeant Lynch was here?' She shook her head. Cole looked at the other drinkers but they kept their heads down. He lifted a copy of the Racing Post, set himself to studying the form. He saw the bargirl look up as the door opened. Lynch. The policeman's face covered in old acne scars like a mask of affliction.

'John Cole. Ministry of Defence. We talked on the phone.'

'I hear tell you're looking into the body.'

'You hear right. The body and the dumping.'

'What's your interest?'

'A body found on what might be Ministry land. A possible crime.'

'There's no evidence so far that the girl was the victim of a crime. Can you confirm that the land belongs to the MOD?'

'I intend to. Has the body been identified?'

'Female between the ages of sixteen and twenty-five. Doesn't fit any listed missing person. We're looking at historic.'

'Where is she?'

'Who?'

'The dead girl.'

'Where do they put dead people?'

'The morgue.'

'Then that's where she is.'

'Is it open?'

'Only if you're dead.'

'Who's in charge?'

'The mortician is Morgan.'

'What investigations are being carried out?'

'An inquest is scheduled for next Monday.'

'Why wait so long?'

'She's been down there long enough. She'll wait awhile. There's been samples took. They'll wait for them to come back from the lab. They want to establish how long she's been in the ground before they use the knife on her.'

She's been down there long enough. The girl lost in the strata, the deep undertow of the sand.

'What about the lorries doing the dumping?'

'They've been coming in on the ferry, going straight back out again. There's no way to track them down.'

'Somebody must have seen something.'

'There's a woman lives on her own out on the Limekiln road,' Lynch said. 'She made a complaint about lorries at night. Artics. Putting the hammer down. No lights. No one paid her any heed.'

'No investigation?'

'We thought she was dreaming,' Lynch said, 'she doesn't recall much. The clutch has slipped.'

'What do you mean the clutch has slipped?'

'A stroke or something like it. A cerebral event, Mr Cole. She's as smart as a whip they say, but she can't talk right. The words come out wrong. She was left at the altar after the war and she hasn't been right since.'

'Left at the altar?'

'In the forties. An airman. He never came back. It happened around here.'

'What about forensics?'

'A scene of crime team come down from HQ.'

'They examined the scene?'

'They stood around looking at the hole in the ground and

says to me what do you think we can tell from that? Not very much says I, and they agreed.'

'They take samples as well?'

'We don't have the time nor the money to be analysing filth from a hole in the ground for them that's been dead fifty years, they says.'

'I didn't know there was a time limit, Sergeant.'

'They put on the white suits right enough and examined the ground, but it was churned up with men's boots and lorry tracks. They done their duty. What would be there fifty-odd years after she died?'

Cole followed Lynch out onto the quay. A north-east wind blew up the boat channel. Hanks of net twine blew through the harbour margins, caught on discarded trawl cable. There were scattered fish scales, marine diesel spills. A white box van was parked at the inner basin. A group of women stood in the lee of the ice plant. They each held a leather-bound hymnal. Men in black suits took speakers dressed in black cloth from the rear of the van and set them on tripods. A portable harmonium was handed over the wall and placed between the speakers. The men moved deliberately. They regarded themselves as elect. A girl stood apart from the women with her back to the outer basin. She wore a floral skirt which touched the ground. She had on a white cap. Her fringe was gathered under it and her hair fell to her waist at the back.

The women wore long dresses buttoned to the throat. They wore no make-up. They seemed to have come from a latter century, pilgrim wives. An elder sat down to the harmonium.

The voices of the women coming across the harbour. This was the hymnal of the town, the voices cadenced, God-haunted. The girl joined the other women, her back half-turned. The oldest man beckoned to her to put her hair under the cap. Upritchard.

'Who are they?'

'The Elected Brethren.'

'Look like they belong in history.'

'Some of them.'

'Not all?'

'I'm one of them.'

Morne Hospital

The hospital stood on the high ground above the river. It had been built on the site of the town workhouse and the workhouse graveyard stood on the river below the hospital. Ungraven stone markers beneath the scrub grass.

The hospital building was closed save for the morgue. War-time Nissen huts in the hospital grounds served as the old people's home for the infirm of the town and its hinterland. Cole could see residents in wingback chairs in the closed-in glass porch. Bone-thin, palsied.

A hearse was parked behind the quarters of the old. The undertaker Morgan wore a black tailcoat and top hat at the wheel, a carnival barker's attire, peddling an underhand burlesque. There'd be something behind canvas only shown after dark, some whimpering thing lying in the straw. He opened the car window to Cole, his eyes fixed straight ahead.

'The old in this place act like bloody royalty,' Morgan said, 'and them the leavings of the town.'

'The leavings of the town?'

'Put names to every one of them, seed, breed and generation. They think they're on the brink of salvation but they're not.'

The old people seemed imperious to Cole, a peerage of their kind. One of them lifted a hand to the car.

'After the war the hospital was all sorts. Ambulance station. Children's home. Old people's home. Then they parked the geriatrics in the huts. The place is closed, falling down.' Morgan pointed to the portico of the main hospital building. Part of the plaster had fallen away from the inside wall to show the granite rubble construction behind.

'There's a smell of chemicals off your dead girl.'

'What kind of chemicals?'

'Formaldehyde. It may be that the formalin was part of the hospital waste.'

'I don't know what that is.'

'Dilute formaldehyde. It's a preservative and bactericide. Histology labs use it for keeping organ samples. Undertakers keep gallon flagons. When you're done you can't just tip them down the drain. If some of that has been dumped on top of her, the body would keep. Complicates the autopsy process.'

'How soon will you know how long the body has been there?'

'I don't know. Wesley Upritchard is anxious to know as well. He owns part of the land. Wants the Ministry to own the rest of it. Lets him off the hook.'

'Off the hook?'

'It lets him off the hook with regard to having a recent

corpse on his rotten property. Doesn't absolve him of anything else.'

'He's a minister. Absolution should come natural.'

'Upritchard and his pals ran this town since the war. That's a lot of sinning.'

'Can I see her?'

'That's court business, mister. You need to apply for an order.'

Cole imagined he could smell the formalin now, the chemical stink working its way into the neural pathways. He felt as if cold hands were dragging him down into some elaborate devising of the underworld.

In the car he took a photograph from his pocket. The photo had been printed on bromide paper in greyscale. The top left-hand corner creased and the surface spotted with brown damp marks but the two boys are clear enough. One sits at a metal-framed wooden desk, the other stands behind, a teenager, posed with his hand on the sitting boy's shoulder. The younger boy is smiling, gap-toothed. The older boy looks solemn. The world on his shoulders. They are both wearing grey school shorts. The older boy's jumper is frayed at the cuffs. Both are wearing black shoes that look too big and heavy for their thin, white legs. You think rickets, slum diseases. There is a heavy cast-iron radiator in the background, the floors stone-flagged. The photograph token of a promise made.

Cole parked in the Hollow behind the Roxboro Hotel. The river in flood. Debris on the margins. Water in choked drains, the sucking darkness. The far bank in blackness. Slum clearances here thirty years ago, the site levelled. Children with diphtheria. His room was at the rear of the building, looking out over the Hollow and beyond that the roofs of the town, the streetlights glowing like naphtha, giving way to the shadows of old entryways, back yards, the town's unslept gothic. A rainsquall blown in from the sea darkened the town.

He walked across the car park. Two girls were outside the off licence. They wore coloured blouses in pink and blue which stood out like damask in the stark yard. Two boys stood in the lee of the dancehall gable, shoulders hunched against the driven blast. Cole wondered what they waited on for there seemed no prospect of anything other than more rain, more night.

Three

The security camera outside the Lighthouse cafe is tilted towards the oldest caravan in the park, its rust-streaked cladding and tyres sunk to the axle in the sand. Kay's caravan. The step up is an upturned crate. The curtains are hung on plastic-covered wire and do not close properly, so that sometimes Kay can be glimpsed passing close to the window.

A Hitachi jeep pulls up. Wesley Upritchard walks straight to the door. He doesn't look around. He's gone beyond that level of furtiveness. The door opens as he reaches it. The camera records a woman's bare arm holding the door handle. Kay's arm. Then the door closes and the camera frames the caravan, sand rustling in the chassis, marram grass bent over in the wind.

Kay had just showered. A towel wrapped around her head, her blouse and skirt for the next day ironed. Bathed and shriven in a white bathrobe. There was a smell of nail varnish remover, a bottle of cleanser and cotton wool on the Formica table.

'This caravan should be scrapped. It lowers the tone.'

'I didn't know there was a tone. What do you want, Minister Upritchard? I paid the rent.'

'I'm not here for that. You know about the sandpit?'

'About the body they found? Of course. I saw the police and undertaker there.'

'What did you hear about it?'

'All I heard is that they found a body.'

'You've been gathering stuff from the war. All things best left alone.'

'It's the reason I'm here. Uniforms and things. The library exhibition.'

'They're saying the body's from the wartime. Some local girl got in trouble with an American soldier during the war. He took off and she threw herself into the sandpit in her despair.'

'Is that what they're saying?'

'She wouldn't be the first around here did it. She got what she deserved perhaps. The wages of sin.'

'High wages, Minister. Who was the man came round today?'

'Ministry of Defence lawyer. Says that the body might have been found on their ground.'

'Was it?'

'It could be. None of it is mine anyway. I have willed it to the congregation. To the Brethren.'

Upritchard turned to her, his hands held palm-upwards in appeal. He was surrendering his life bounty. The failing business, the corrupted ground. He was a forlorn elder in a black suit. Kindly, misunderstood.

'I'll leave you in peace.'

'Peace would suit both of us, Reverend. I got to visit someone.'

'Who?'

'An old woman lives on the Limekiln road.'

'Lily.'

'Yes.'

'She has not been in her right mind for many years.'

'They say she was in love with an airman. He got lost in the war.'

'Plenty of people got lost in the war. Who put you on to her?'

'That would be telling.'

'There's things best left alone.'

'Somebody always says that.'

'And maybe they're right.'

'Maybe, Reverend. For the moment you're on your own with a half-dressed woman in a caravan and she's asking you to leave.'

'Give my regards to Lily. Tell her I was asking for her.'

'I might.'

The Chalets, Limekiln Road

Kay pulled up outside a line of holiday chalets with flat tarred roofs built along the Limekiln road. The place an essay in the temporary. The paint had been stripped from the chalets by wind and salt and the wooden fronts had silvered and warped. The front gardens were unkempt. Marram grass grew through the fence stakes.

The Limekiln road. No place for a woman to live on her own. No place for anyone to live on their own. The road running along the sea's edge. At night the east wind rattles the dry stems in the reed beds. In the dark there is the call of seabirds from the mudflats, eerie pipings carried across the shifting channels and tide races. Brackish drains carry run-off into the shallows. Dead alder trees on the verges. People come out from the town to dump on the scrublands.

The doctor said that the chalets were not suitable for an elderly woman but Lily knew that they were the only place. A location for all that had failed, clung to without reason or hope. The wind found the unplanked spaces, the shrunken doorjambs, coming up through the floorboards. There were rustlings in the foundations. Dead shrubs rattled against the windowpanes. The substance of the house was probed by the night and found wanting. There were roof spaces, hollow stud walls, cavities, voids.

Inside the front door, the prayer book on the hall stand. Blown sand carried through the hall door and onto the lino-leum. Kay called Lily's name into the darkness.

They sat in the lean-to kitchen. Rain on the corrugated roof above their heads. Kay watched Lily put out her tea at a steel-framed table with a red Formica top. Lily eating austere meals, the radio on in the corner, a cracked transistor playing country. The back door strained against its hinges as though something sought entry. Lily said never turn your back on the sea. It was not a thing to be liked. There were kelpies, mourn-ful voices. You had to beware. You could be drawn down into the faithless depths.

Kay went upstairs and into the bedroom, pushing aside the curtain that hung in the doorway. Rain beat upon the roof. You could feel the walls flex in the wind, the windows loose in their frames, shantytown sounds.

Kay started to fix Lily's bedding. Folding and tucking. Firming things, smoothing and easing. Lily followed her.

'They found a body. Word is someone who took their own life years ago,' Kay said.

'I hear.' Lily's unstructured sentences resonating in the cold night. Words had long ago started to slip away from Lily. They no longer attached themselves to things. Household items all around her, eerie and nameless.

'A woman. They're saying from the war.'

'War take people. War die them.'

'The poor girl.'

'Naked her?'

'The girl? Was she dressed you mean? I don't know.'

'Come bare world go bare world.'

'I hope not, Lily.'

'Lonesome her.'

'I know. Time for bed.'

Lily rose and went to the window. She opened the curtains and looked across the lough shore to the dark mass of the aerodrome.

'What are you doing?'

'Look sky. Look day, look night.'

'What are you looking for?'

'Oscar Tango Bravo.'

'I wish I knew what you meant sometimes.'

Kay came over and stood beside her. She felt Lily's head against her cheek, the feathered texture of her grey hair, her frame light-boned as though she readied herself for the air so that if Kay opened the window the old woman would float beyond her, out over the starless lough. There were lights moving on the sand dunes on the other side of the water. Hunters from the city lamping hares in the marram grass.

The Lighthouse Cafe, Pirnmill

The cafe is at the entrance to the caravan park. Blown sand piles against the seaward side. A wooden-framed building with a bitumen roof, the wood seams shrunken, its window frames loose, rattling in the east wind blowing up the channel. The cafe has been closed for several years. The wind has scoured the painted signs. Ices. Soft drinks.

Upritchard's jeep is parked outside the front door. A security camera above the door, the kind of camera you get in a small business. Grey-cased, tilted. Cabling stapled to the wall. There is dust on the lens, accumulated grime on the plastic.

Inside tables and chairs have been stacked to one side of the cafe. The beech planking on the floor has gapped and sprung. The glass counter top is covered with dust and sand. A cake stand lies on its side in a display case. Upritchard catches sight of himself in the specked mirror behind the counter. He looks furtive, shambling. He goes into the office behind the counter. It is late. Upritchard doesn't sleep well.

The camera cabling runs to a box on a shelf. There are boxes of receipts, used till rolls. A green light flashing on the video recorder. The recorder is on a twenty-four-hour loop. The tape erases itself and starts again. The footfall of the years stored then wiped out. The mounting has shifted so that you can't see people's faces. The customers, the ticket sellers, summer visitors, coming and going in silence, winter coats giving way to shirtsleeves then the autumn again and when the door opens dead leaves whirl through the door darkly. The ghost images overlaid again and again.

Upritchard stares at the camera. He has been lay preacher of the Elected Brethren since the Reverend Davidson died. He knows he is unworthy of the role. He has never married. Unworthy of that as well. This is as near as he has ever got, at spy on the summer visitors, girls undressing in the dunes, couples in parked cars after dark. The camera fixed on the librarian's caravan now. Leaves blow across the frame, reed fragments. There is turbulence off-screen. Easterlies blowing into the mouth of the lough. Clouds race. A swell beats against the shingle and the sand dunes. Someone moves into the frame, wearing a long coat, collar pulled up, the figure along the caravan siding towards the window supported by one hand, the face turned towards the caravan window. The curtains are closed but there was a blade of light showing and the figure outside pressed their face against the window at that point, both hands against the window, covetous of what the interior held, the women space. A gust of wind rocks the caravan and the cowled figure moves with the wind, drifting out of frame. Upritchard steps back. A figure of the night from an old tale, cloaked, revenant. When he looks again the frame is empty.

Four

The chalets were set back from the road. Two storeys with old shedding to the rear. Cole went to the front door and knocked. He waited for it to be answered. He looked across the bay. The bents and shallows exposed at low tide showed the concrete stands of aerodrome landing lights, the rusted baseplates of the light gantries still visible. A freighter rode out the tide at the mouth of the channel, deck lights blazing.

He saw a woman at a side window of the porch. Her pale, shrunken face hung in the glass. She stepped clear of the window and opened the door. She wore a tweed skirt and a green blouse closed at the neck with a brooch.

'My name is Cole. I represent the Ministry of Defence. I'm looking into events at the aerodrome.'

'Found girl.'

'A body was found, yes.'

'Oscar Tango Bravo.'

'I heard you saw lorries on the Limekiln road?'

'Come with no lights them lorries. Maybe dream them.'

'They weren't a dream. How many?'

'No one ask Lily, no one tell.'

'You reported it?'

'Tell Lynch. Bad article.'

'He said nothing?'

'Says Lily afraid out here on her own. Care home for Lily he says, keep your silly beak shut.'

'You don't want to be put into a home. Lynch was threatening you with it?'

'Lily not afraid.'

'If you say so.'

'I say so.'

'Lonely here though.'

'Lily not lonely. Has Kay.'

'Who's Kay?'

'Library girl. Listen.'

'Listen for what?'

Lily's been waiting for the planes for many years, her Oscar Tango Bravo, the sound of the engines coming back off the mountain. The heavy motor sound, labouring through the map contours. Navigator crouched in the bay. Wingtips iced from eight hours at thirty-five thousand feet. Minus eighteen on the fuselage. Coming in from Gander and Newfoundland, the frozen bases, flying on auxiliary tanks light on ballast and no payload, the controls light, the pilot's eyes on the altimeter, for the updraught will carry the aircraft a thousand feet either direction in seconds.

Cole followed her eyes out to the bay. The mountains enclose the lough, form a canyon, the air currents shifting. A side wind you thought you'd imagined alters your bearing seven or eight degrees.

Lily sees it the way it was fifty-five years ago. The landing lights coming on at night, a V shape pointing towards the main runway opening up in front of them, the light skein seen from three miles out at two thousand feet. Cole only sees used shotgun cartridges half-sunk in the machair channels. The reed beds shifting in the wind. Beyond the reed beds the mud shallows and the channel empty of shipping.

When Lily looked again Cole was gone.

The Library, Morne Esplanade

Dusk on the Esplanade. A man in a raincoat made his way alone by the iron railings and past the front steps of the library. Cole. The red sandstone darkened by salt wind blown up from the tide. Dark wood, heavy wrought-iron spouting detached and crooked. The annexe roof showed wooden laths where loose slates had been carried off in western gales. The windows shiver in loose putty, the frames decayed. A facade of sombre purpose, that purpose now lost. Cole put his hand to the brass door handle, stained green where sea spray had corroded it. The interior hallway was dim, the lights covered with dust. The lending desk stood at the entrance to the book room. Kay standing with her hands on the dark wood as though she were about to testify.

'I'd like to speak to the librarian.'

'I'm the only person working here.'

'I'm looking for some information on the aerodrome. My name is Cole. I'm from the Ministry of Defence.'

'What do you want, Mr Cole?'

'I need to see anything you have on the original land purchase of the aerodrome.'

'You'd be better looking at the register of deeds. This isn't a legal depository.'

'I intend to look but the land maps may not be conclusive.'

'I think we have the original land maps and compulsory purchase orders.'

'Are they available to view?'

'Yes. Not that anyone ever does. They should have been transferred out of here long since but nobody is interested. So you're here about the land, not that poor girl.'

'Dead girls aren't my area. What do you know about her?'

'Nothing.'

'It's just a question.'

'Then why do I feel like I'm standing in a witness box?'

'I don't know.'

'The building was a courthouse before it was a library.'

'Maybe that's it.'

'Maybe.'

'If I asked you to tell the whole truth and nothing but the truth, would that help?'

'No. Nobody tells the whole truth about anything round here.'

'Even under oath?'

'Especially. But I'm not under oath, am I?'

'Of course not. Can I see the records now?'

'You can have a few hours, until nine.'

'It'll be a start.'

'There are a lot of records down there.'

'I'm used to looking in archives.'

*

A metal staircase with a wooden balustrade led down to the records room and offices in the basement. Cole followed Kay down into the basement area, the dim-lit realm. Forty-watt bulbs in dusty storerooms. They walked along a steel gantry. The stairway caged in one-inch wire mesh. Her shoes rang on the metalwork. He watched their shadows on the wall. Her shadow upright, his looking bent and crabbed as though malice followed her into the deep places of the building. Withdrawn library books in cardboard cartons were left on the metal steps. The corridor was bare whitewash with glossed pipework leading to the furnace room.

'Most of the town records are here. Court documents. Medical records. You can't remove anything.'

'I won't need to at the moment.'

'Here.'

'What's this?'

'Wartime map. It might be relevant.'

Cole waited until she climbed the stairs then he closed the records room door behind him.

He turned on the interior light and spread the wartime land map on his knee. Smelling of old inks, long-gone printing processes. The map legend inked in on the margins. Hangars and hardstandings in the centre of the map, the accommodation blocks. The other buildings scattered over the area, working outwards from the centre to the sparse buildings at the perimeter, the salt margins of marram grass and sand, the east wind blowing through the chain-link fencing. He looked at the dates and the transfers of title. Upritchard's statement was confirmed. The MOD had maintained ownership of a quarter acre at the bottom of Upritchard's property.

He let the map fall and looked to the filing cabinets in ranks leading to the darkness at the back of the room where the lightbulbs had failed. He counted down the years, moving into the shadows.

Some of the cabinets had fallen over and the files were on the ground. He moved one with his foot. Medical records dated October 1979. The front of the file stamped 'Confidential'. He lifted the cover. The patient's name and file number were at the top of the page. Below that the doctor's name. He pushed between the cabinets. It was hard to read the typed inserts on the filing cabinet drawers now. The cellar wall beside him made of brickwork painted white, damp seeping through the mortar, the air foetid. He opened a drawer and took out a file. White mould grew on the cardboard cover, the paper within the cover damp. He read the patients' dates of birth, ages. He looked at the medical notations. Measles. Dystrophy. Melanoma. Broken limbs. A bundle of death certificates. Tuberculosis. Succumbed to diphtheria. Thrown from quarry machinery. Stillborn. Lost overboard, presumed drowned. The mortal doings of the place ledgered and left to silence and decay. The death trove of the town.

Back here in the darkness, the filing cabinet drawers unyielding, rusted. Leaning together like old stones.

The records he was looking for were against the back wall in two long black cabinets. When he tried them they were locked but he braced his feet against the wall and pulled at the handle so that the front piece came away from the drawer frame and the documents inside were exposed. The files deteriorated, the documents almost illegible. He'd have to piece things together, gather the fragments. He laid the documents against the cast-iron radiator to dry.

Cole found Kay in an adjacent storeroom putting up a wire mannequin. She took a battledress top from its box.

'I'm trying to get a whole uniform. Olive-green drabs.'

'A uniform?'

'It's for an exhibition. Wartime. The Americans in training for D-Day. Forty thousand of them came through here, soldiers and airmen. General Patton gave a speech at the aerodrome.'

'You wouldn't know.'

'They don't talk about the war years here. They leave bin bags of material at the door. At least someone does. Other things I get from thrift shops.'

He disliked thrift shops, going through the effects of the dead. You felt you would come across something you recognised, something scuffed, worn at the elbows, some threadbare presence that once was yours. A smell of must from the bag contents, a smell of back cupboards and attics. She turned off the light. He followed her upstairs.

'Any contact with the American side of it?'

'None of them ever came back here, far as I know. Eighteen-, nineteen-year-olds. Most of them died.' She turned away and looked out of the foyer window as if their lives might be out there somewhere, boyhoods adrift in the incendiary night.

Kay watched Cole leave, the wind catching his gabardine as he opened the door, dead leaves whirling across the parquet until the door closed and the darkness beyond it claimed him.

33

She closed the front doors and deadlocked them, the court clerk's brass tag still attached to the key. She turned off the lights in the reading rooms and set the thermostat. She descended the iron gantry to the records level. Cole had not turned off the fluorescent light in the records room. The records he had examined were placed on the reading desk, files in brown cardboard sleeves, dated and annotated in pen on the front sleeve. In the corridor outside an iron pipe creaked. They didn't feel to her like transcripts of the past but of the doings of the town foretold. It was what they taught. Everything was written in the book. Everything was ordained.

She crossed the street to Mrs Orr. The charity shop owner expecting her. Kay at home here with the rummage, knowing you were dealing in the effects of the dead. She liked to move among the racks of clothing hung tight together. Suitcases. Broken household goods. The shops tended by elderly women, sisters to the gloom. They were the keepers of artefacts and sisters of last charity. They held office among the lost things of the world.

The thrift shop had been a Post Office, the cashier's position now shuttered and dust-covered, its brass bars tarnished, clothing baled on the worn counter.

'Some of the Yanks left a bit of themselves behind,' Mrs Orr said.

'What do you mean?'

'There's many the woman lay with a Yank is what I'm saying.'

'I'm only putting on a display. What they did is their own business.'

'It'd be better if you let things be.'

'People are interested.'

'People's interested in many the thing. Doesn't mean you have to give it to them.'

Magazines and newspapers were bundled at the rear of the shop. People left in old scrapbooks. Family albums. Family groups on sun-dazzled beaches. Damp stains on the emulsions, the paper spotted and foxed. Kay thought of the settings without them. The unpeopled beachfronts scoured by the wind, the overgrown beauty spots. Where had they gone, the mothers in angular sunglasses and arcane swimming costumes, the children with concave chests?

There were celluloid buttons. Stockings with pinked seams. Rayon fabric. Stockings in American brown, laddered and mended with nail polish. Thread of utility quality. Black patent shoes with a Cuban heel. There was an aluminium film canister under the black patent shoes, dented, the metal dulled and scratched. Kay opened the can to the spindled film inside, the smell of old developing fluid rising from it.

'What's this?'

'It come from the man owned the cinema. McKee. When he died his daughter left it in. Says she was well rid of it, and well rid of him along with it. Brethren. Thought they owned the town.'

'I'll give you five for it.'

'You need a projector.'

'It's super eight. I got one.'

'I got something else for you,' Mrs Orr said. 'Somebody left it in a black bag at the library door. I lifted it so it wouldn't get wet.'

'Did you see who left it?'

'Seen nothing except the rain. I took it out of the bag and dried it.'

Kay took the dress uniform from her. The dark olive wool garment. More formal than she thought. The garrison cap fitted under the epaulette. Brass buttons and webbed belt. The uniform jacket. She ran her fingers along the seamed pockets to see if it had been worn. The stitching frayed on the belt end, the brass buckle scored, the corners worked into with Brasso. There were dark patches on each shoulder where regimental insignia had been removed. She looked for laundry marks on the lining of the battledress jacket but there were none.

'Are you going to take it or are you going to have an inquest on it?' Mrs Orr said.

'I wonder who he was?' Kay said.

'Whoever he is, he's long gone anyhow,' Mrs Orr said. Kay took the uniform from her. It was heavier than she had expected. As if part of the human weight of the man that had worn it had been retained, as if what she held was weighted down with presence, the once-loved form.

*

Next morning Cole was standing in the doorway of the library when she arrived. Wearing his raincoat over a suit. Grey hair cut short. He looked like bad news. She unlocked the door.

'Where's your office?'

'What?'

'Your law office.'

'Shotts. Scotland.'

'The blooming heather.'

'Closed down mines. Closed down foundries. The prison. Not much to look at bar the slag heaps.'

'How long are you going to be at those files?'

'Until I find what I'm looking for. A few days. There's the inquest on Monday as well.'

'I'm lonesome thinking about her. Not even a name.'

'She has a name, they just haven't found it yet.'

The bundled files had dried on the hot pipes. There was an unwholesome smell in the air, old moulds, drifting spores. Cole put the dried files on the desk. He started to work through them. The pages had adhered to each other and he had to pull them apart, putting each page on the desk in front of him. He thought of himself in a dim-lit archive, bent over old manuscripts, found objects, the pages fragile and discoloured. Patients suffering from pleurisy, distempers. A child was reported to have died from an infestation of ringworm to the skull.

The medical files had been stored together. They were not in order of name or date. He knew that Reay's should be among them but he took care with the other files, putting them along the wall in order. The dead and the halt must be given their due. It was late afternoon before he found Reay's medical file, the cardboard folder empty.

Five

Davis said it was funny that Hooper had wanted to be a pilot.

'Begging your pardon, Hooper, but they hardly let a man of colour drive a motor car never mind fly a plane.'

'I liked the idea of flying, getting into the air.'

'You'll get into the air all right. At the end of the hangman's rope.'

In spring 1939 Hooper had got a job in a Negro cinema beside Dobbins Field in Atlanta. During the day he would sit on the galvanised roof of the cinema and watch plane traffic. Corsairs and P-38s coming in low and fast at strafing height, silvered and banking. The *Courier Times* said they were destined for aircraft carriers in Hawaii. Hooper thought of them locked in mortal combat high above the palm trees, the atolls and shimmering waters.

Unknown aircraft came in from the north. There were airbases in the Arctic Circle. World of Wonder magazine talked about bases deep in the permafrost regions. It made Hooper cold to think of it.

Hooper cut out a photograph of Charles Lindbergh from Time magazine and stuck it to the barn wall. Lindbergh was wearing a flying helmet and a leather jacket with a sheepskin collar. You could see the fatigue, his face lined, the lines grimed with engine oil. His eyes looked beyond, to far-off aerial combats. Lindbergh had skimmed across the underside of storm clouds, the world roofed with ice. He had flown across the Atlantic wave tops, spume on the windscreen of the Spirit of St Louis. When Hooper was in trouble he thought of Lindbergh, the airman in his mind the day he met his defence counsel.

'My name is Captain Bernard Phair. I will be your advocate in the matter of your general court martial.'

'I never done anything, Sir.'

'Let's stay with the matter in hand. Please state your name, rank and unit.'

'Hooper. Private Gabriel Hooper.'

'Private Hooper. The prosecution says that you knowingly and wilfully lay in wait—'

'I know what the prosecution says, Sir.'

'The charge against you carries a capital sentence.'

'I heard that.'

'A capital sentence means that the death penalty applies.'

'You don't be long getting to know that around here, Sir. They tell you right and quick. But I never done anything.'

'Your statement says you did.'

'I never said any of them things.'

'You signed the confession.'

'I was ordered to sign that paper by the base commander, Sir.'

'Do you deny that you knew Miss Davidson?'

'That don't prove nothing.'

'Were you intimate with Miss Davidson?'

'I'd rather not say, Sir.'

'That attitude won't help.'

'It's the only attitude I got, Sir.'

'They have other evidence against you.'

'What other evidence?'

'They searched your locker at Pirnmill.'

'I know they did. I was there.'

'They found soiled clothing belonging to a female.'

'Then somebody put it there.'

'It doesn't sound very likely. My advice, plead guilty. Throw yourself on the mercy of the court.'

'And get hanged. Don't sound like mercy to me.'

'You are entitled to request that a third of the court consist of enlisted men. I wouldn't be inclined to do that. It turns the rest of the court against you. Besides, it probably wouldn't do you any good.'

'Because I'm coloured.'

'There's that defiance again, Private. It won't do you any good in court.'

'I'm not sure what will, Sir.'

'I can't help you if you don't help yourself.'

'They didn't take down the scaffold.'

'What?'

'They didn't take down the scaffold, Sir, after they hanged Martinez. That's what they usually do. Take down the scaffold and rebuild it next time they need it, Sir.'

'Hooper?'

'Was there a silver half-dollar in the locker?'

'I don't know. I don't think so.'

'There should of been a silver half-dollar in the locker.'

'Not that I know of. And I wouldn't bring it up. They wouldn't take kindly to an accusation of stealing because that's what it sounds like. Make things worse than they already are. You have already got a conviction in the States for trespass.'

'I only wanted to see a proper plane, Sir.'

Dobbins Air Force Base, Atlanta
September 1939

Hooper went in under the wire after the late screening that evening. He just wanted to be brought up against the fabric of the aircraft, the actual matter of it. The plane parked close to the perimeter. It came in on the first of September. They said that Charles Lindbergh had flown it. It looked like a spy plane built to drift in the ionosphere, blown to the edge of what was known by eerie solar winds. The wings were long and spindly, the pilot and navigator in a Perspex bubble. It carried complex aerial arrays under its nose. Camera pods were slung under the wings. You thought about men who would sit apart from others, who carried the silence of near space with them. They had been on the edge of the world and had not come back unchanged. It flew slowly in a grid pattern over the aerodrome. The noise of the engines was carried out to sea so that it seemed soundless, as though summoned from some other world.

Up close the silver fuselage was dented and oxidised. He put his hand against the dinged alloys, the riveted panels with black exhaust deposits in the crevices. Climbing the fold-down ladder and entering the fuselage. Getting the kerosene tang of aviation fuel, lubricant smells. The cockpit door was open. He could see the banked dials, altimeters, odometers. The heavy controls for flap and rudder, for loft and tilt. A pilot's overalls and a leather flying helmet hung behind the navigator's table.

He sat in the pilot's seat and placed the earphones over his ears. Charlie Zulu to control tower. The flight-deck argot. Beneath his feet the miles of piping, fuel lines, the deep hydraulics to drive the flaps and rudder.

He realised why wind speeds were calculated in knots, why they used the maritime term, the hewn-out, salt-tempered word. There were the fastnesses of the air, the swirling treacheries of ten-thousand-foot-high air columns. There were currents, sudden windshear, buffeted on high.

He felt the plane flex on its undercarriage. Someone climbing the ladder. A man's face in the doorway, then another. A torch beam played on the instrument panel. He saw the peaked caps and he knew who they were. They were the end of dreaming.

'Looks like we got a Jap spy here.'

'Black boy was about to take off in this here plane.'

'Them East Atlanta boys got their own air force now.'

'This here's United States Air Force property, son. They'll be aiming to get it fumigated now.'

'Let's get a look at him. See what he stole.'

Hands pulled him from the pilot's seat. His leg caught and twisted under the rudder pedal.

Hooper wanted Lindbergh to be there. His face would be in shadow. He would speak with a drawl. He would take

Hooper around the plane, a hand placed around his shoulders, explaining how the wings worked for lift and together they would catch the sweet winds.

Captain Phair placed the file on the table between them. He looked like he wanted to be somewhere else, Hooper told Davis that night. 'I can't say I blame him. I wanted to be somewhere else myself.'

'All the depositions have been received, the witness testimonies. The physical evidence has been transported from Belfast and will be available to the prosecution.'

'Don't any of these people have to come to the court martial and speak for their own selves, Sir?'

'No. The depositions are sufficient.'

'Can't you ask questions of the witnesses then, Sir?'

'This is a court martial, not a civilian courtroom. Different standards apply.'

'I never done it, Sir.'

'There must be some evidence you can bring forward in your own defence. Just saying you didn't do it isn't enough.'

'Isn't nothing to be said but the truth. Is what my grandma used to say.'

'Spare me the homespun wisdom, son. Your grandma isn't on trial for her life. Can you explain the garments found in your locker?'

'I know nothing about them garments.'

'Intimate garments.'

'I don't know how they got there.'

'Item one. A lady's stockings and suspender belt. Item two. A lady's brassiere. You want me to go on?'

'No.'

'Can you explain their presence in your quarters?'

'No Sir, I cannot.'

'You better think of something before Monday, Hooper.'

'I can't think of nothing, Sir.'

'Have you got your letters, Hooper?'

'Yes, Sir.'

'You got folks?'

'My grandma.'

'Can she read? Because if she can I suggest you write to her and tell her what has happened. Only don't say anything in the letter you wouldn't say in open court.'

'She can read, Sir.' She could read infidelity in a man's face. She knew the wages of sin and the specie it was paid in. She could read anvil lightning on the horizon.

Hooper told Davis about the evidence.

'What garments is them?'

'They found these clothes belonging to the girl in my locker.'

'You put them there? Take a souvenir?'

'No, I never took a souvenir.'

'You know the girl?'

'Met her at a dance.'

'You give her a charver, the old dog and bone?'

'Ain't none of your business.'

'It's going to be the whole world's business in that court-room. Still and all, if you says you never done the deed then me, I have to take your word for it. Necromancy might be what we're looking at here.'

'Necromancy?'

'The dark arts.'

'I wish you wouldn't talk like that, Davis.'

'I'm dead serious, Hooper. Stranger things have happened. You ever look at a dollar bill, Hooper? You see the eye and the pyramid on it? World's ruled by Masons and the like. Me and youse nothing to them.'

'Shut up, Davis,' Hooper said. But the image would not leave him. The pyramid and the lidless eye above it. God-less. Floating. That night Lindbergh came unbidden into Hooper's sleep but when he tried to look at the pilot's face under his cap there was nothing there but darkness.

Six

Pirnmill Aerodrome
22nd November 2000

Cole stood at the edge of the pit. There were groups of aerodrome buildings in the distance. Lone outposts. Locals had tried to find purposes for the runways and hardstandings. The caravan park on the seaward side. The blockworks. A disused kart track, the course marked out in old tyres. In places the concrete of the runway had been torn up and formed into walls.

Upritchard was watching. Cole laid out the land map on the ground and weighed it down with stones at each corner. He drove a stake into the ground at the perimeter corner of the main runway and measured. He knew it to be a charade to conceal his true purpose in the town from Upritchard, but he did it properly in the knowledge that he had spent much of his life looking for boundaries that were not there. Upritchard did not conceal himself. He wanted Cole to know he was there, a harried figure, isolated, cloud building on the mountain behind him.

'That'll never stand up in court,' Upritchard said.

'It doesn't have to,' Cole said. 'This is preliminary. We'll send a surveyor out for legal purposes. The Ministry won't pay for a survey at this stage.'

'Sergeant says it's a wartime death. An accident, he says.'

'Maybe. The autopsy will tell us one way or another. Any girls go missing around here during the war years?'

'Mister, any number of girls went missing. Went running after a soldier's uniform and never came back.'

Upritchard stood over the map. He did not think of the place as charted. He did not think it could be charted. The ground adrift under the aerodrome concrete, the alluvial drifts.

'Just because she turned up under a man's land doesn't mean she started out there.'

'That's not the way the court will see it.'

'I could bring in experts.'

'Experts cost money.'

'You'll tell me what you found.'

'I'll tell the Ministry. It'll be up to them to tell you or not tell you.'

They watched Lynch's car approach along the perimeter road, concrete dust raised behind it. Lynch stopped and got out. Cole walked towards him. Upritchard stood his ground. He could do no other.

'The Reverend Upritchard says you're trespassing on his land.'

'If he's a reverend why does he have land?'

'He's a lay minister. It's the way the Elected Brethren work.'

'They're elected now, are they?'

'Elected by God. In their own heads anyhow.'

'What are you saying, Sergeant?'

'I'm suggesting you pull back. Let Minister Upritchard produce his title deeds and then we'll get a look.'

'I've no objection. I've got what I need anyway.'

'You heading out of town then?'

'I'll wait for the inquest.'

'It's been put off for another few days.'

'For Christ's sakes, Sergeant.'

'Pressure on resources. She can do no harm now anyway.'

'I wasn't thinking about the harm she could do.'

'Will you still stay around?'

'Like I said, Sergeant. Until the autopsy.'

Lynch returned to the station. Upritchard was waiting for him and followed him into the camera room. Lynch fast-forwarded through the early evening customers at the ATM, the shadow people walking jerkily into frame. They looked like characters from early film. The footage scratchy with a look of gone-off film stock. He watched the timeline at the bottom of the frame. Traffic building up at the intersections.

At 5 p.m. the camera outside the library picked up Cole leaving, gathering his coat around him. Cole turned right, crossing the top of the Esplanade.

'Where the hell is he going?'

Cole walked among the others to the corner. People walking head down, their faces turned away from the wind. The town had acquired a behind-the-lines look. Lives eked out in the shadow of loss. Cole turned away from the others as they descended the granite steps towards the Hollow. Cole turned left, towards the old town, cars parked where the Hollow houses had once stood on the river margins, foundations undermined and rotted with floodwater and river vermin, the houses long since demolished.

Lynch switching cameras. Cole walking up Hospital Street. The old town, pavements uneven, houses unroofed and windows empty.

'He's going towards the hospital,' Lynch said. The wind blew debris past Cole on the unpeopled street.

'What does a man like him desire in a place like that?'

'It's all locked up for the night. Empty.'

'Apart from the morgue.'

'It is empty, Upritchard.'

'Does the girl count for nothing?'

'She counted for nothing in her life and now she counts for less.'

'We all count in the eyes of the Lord.'

'Sometimes the Lord looks away, Wesley Upritchard. You know that.'

'What else does Cole do?'

'Walks around the town in the dark. Goes to the harbour.'

'A bad conscience stands in the way of sleep. Is there a security camera at the hospital?'

'Everybody hides something, is that what it is you're saying, Wesley?'

'It rightly is.'

'And me and you is hiding more than most.'

'More than some. Less than others.'

Cole made his way past the housing of the elderly, the Nissen hut curtains pulled against the dark. The wind was blowing from the north and had got up with the onset of the night. The trees had shed their leaves and stood as a formal backdrop to the hospital building. It had not always been a hospital nor had it always been a workhouse. He could see the decorative mouldings on the roofline of the building, the whole thing funereal, a mausoleum to the skeletal girl alone with her rags. He crossed the front of the building and took the old path down the pine slope to the river. The uninscribed grave markers of the workhouse dead visible in the scrub grass at the bottom of the cliff. The pitched tin roof of Kingdom Hall across the river.

Cole went around the back of the hospital to the service buildings. The boiler house. The laundry. Abutments to the main building now doorless, copper piping ripped out for salvage, the roofs sagging. He walked between the buildings, the wind stirring in the tops of the pine trees on the slope down to the river. He moved slowly. He knew what hazards awaited in these townships of the night.

At the rear gable of the hospital he took out a torch and shone it upwards. The light could not be detected from the town and any other eyes that might see it cared only for the dead and the barely living. The torch beam lit the fire escape's tangle of rusted gridwork and fallen iron spouting. Barbed wire had been bent across the fire escape gate but the wire had rotted and he pulled it aside. He kept the torch low and faced to the wall so that anyone who watched would see only a circle of yellow light ascending the gable, a frail diminished sun. The wind moaned in the treetops and fine ice particles stung his face. The metal structure clanked and swayed under his weight. He stopped at the third landing and held the torch on the fire escape door. He saw that the wood surrounding the hasp had filler worked into it and could be levered out. He dug into it with a screwdriver until he had freed the hasp then put his weight against it and forced the door inward.

He closed the door behind him and stood in the corridor at the wing ending. The windows were held in iron frames which had warped over the years, and the bent castings formed reeds which the wind blew across so that you could hear eerie flutings from the rooms leading off the corridor.

The infirmary had been on this wing, and the surgeries. Cole shone the torch on the doors but the brass nameplates had been removed so he pushed each door in turn, shining the light into empty wards stripped of their fittings. The dental surgery was in the centre of the corridor. The dental chair had not been taken, the chrome arms tarnished and the leather seat torn. Water ran in the porcelain spit basin. He ducked his head under the arm of the dentist's light, and the fatigued hydraulic hose of the drill and sluice apparatus touched his face and he flinched away from it. Instruments had been left on a tray on the stainless steel sink. Drill bits and rust-specked scalpel blades, probes and retractors. He took an x-ray plate from the floor and held the torch behind it to show the teeth and the bone housing them, the mouth agape. It felt like a warning. A corpse on a roadside gibbet. A skull set on a post.

The records room stood behind a fireproof door at the rear of the dental surgery. The cabinets were arranged in alphabetical order. The cabinets were not locked but many of the patients' charts had been misfiled. Cole found and removed two charts. He was alone except for the girl in the basement. She was far below him but the distance counted for nothing, nor did the years. He put the files under his jacket and left the building by the fire escape.

Cole met Kay in the Hollow, the files under his raincoat. Her hair was wet. She was carrying a swim bag.

'What are you doing down here?' Kay said.

'I don't sleep well.'

'So you walk.'

'Most nights.'

'What keeps you awake?'

Cole did not answer.

'With me it's the wind. One of these nights it's going to blow my rotten old caravan into the sea.'

'A caravan?'

'It belonged to my parents. I held on to it when they died. I live in it.'

The east wind coming in off the lough. Cole had heard it. He had lain awake to it. At one time it had seemed that there were voices in it.

'It's lonely down here.'

'That's why I like it. Nobody bothers you. The rest of the time there's always somebody watching.'

'You swim?'

'I swam in school. Locals. Nationals. Keeps me fit. I like the pool at night. What about you?'

'I walk.'

'You don't give much away.'

'There's not much to give.'

'Where do you walk in Scotland?'

'Up the valley.'

'Is there a place you go to?'

'There is.'

'What's it called?'

'It's called the Black Laws.'

'Strange name.'

'There are spoil heaps from the pits. From a distance they look like hills.' He spoke a laconic pilgrim language. Plain. Unadorned.

'They'll be talking about us now. The new man in town and the unmarried librarian.'

'They can talk away.'

Easy for you to say, she thought. You don't know this town. She knew Lily's story. To have lain awake in the spinsterish dark assigned to you, your heart growing hard with the years.

'It's cold,' she said.

'It's going to get colder. There will be a storm.'

'How do you know?'

'Because it happened before. A freeze is coming.' He stood before her looking out over the sea. There's a freeze in you, Mister, she thought, and it's calling to whatever is out there.

'Are you any good at fixing things?'

'Depends what.'

'I got an old film. I can't run it until my projector's fixed.'

'I can take a look.'

Kay drove him out through the aerodrome. Past the derelict flight tower and the hangar buildings used now as tyre repair and coachworks, the low mounds of the firing range earthworks to seaward. The buildings gave way to the runway and the hardstandings fenced off from the road. A row of Nissen huts stood near the fence, windowless, sheets of corrugated come adrift to show the narrow girdered framework on the inside. The headlights shone on old bedframes and steel-framed refectory chairs, their canvas seats long rotted.

'Niggertown, they called it,' Kay said, 'where the black GIs lived.'

The buildings fell behind them, derelict neighbourhoods long unpeopled and left to the darkness. A light burned outside the blockworks. Beyond that the gantry raised over the pit where the girl had been found. Sand and spindrift blew across the road in front of the car as they turned down towards the caravan park, an eroded sign for Ocean Sands Caravans turned on its chains. The concrete roadway was pitted with use and marram grass grew through the seams. The caravans were unlit.

'People come here for the holidays and weekends. Place is dead most of the time.'

She parked beside the Lighthouse cafe.

'Everything around here is closed and near falling down,' she said.

They crossed the narrow passage to the caravan. Cole could hear sand blowing against the side panels, the eroding hiss.

'It's a bit of a tip,' she said. She pulled the door open and turned on the light then stood aside to let him in. There was a grace to temporary living, he saw. There was a blue cotton throw over the banquette seating, pieces of driftwood gone white as bone, stones picked from the shingle. A jar of dried sea pinks. A sea urchin casing. The winter sheddings of the ocean. The small cherished objects, all that was wishful, held against the alone. He felt sand on the lino at his feet.

'You'll remember this place if you see it again.'

'Didn't mean to stare.'

'You'd make a good witness at trial. You want tea?'

'All right.'

'Mind the kettle. I need a shower.' She put the projector on the table. He turned it so that he would sit facing out of the windows, looking away from the door to the bedroom and the shower. He heard her go into the bedroom then come out and into the shower.

He worked on the projector, cleaning dust from the vents. He replaced the bulb with one from the box. He could hear the shower water against the bulkhead, the rinse water in the pipe. When he raised his head he saw her dim reflection in the glass, a towel wrapped around her, her shoulders bare, a pale sprite of desire.

He left the table and opened the cupboard under the sink.

'What are you doing?'

'Looking for tinfoil. The fuse is blown.'

'Next time ask.' He took the tinfoil from her and wrapped it around the blown fuse. He plugged it in. There was a smell of hot dust as the bulb warmed. She leaned over him.

The sleeve of her dressing gown touched his face, washed-out cotton smelling of soap. Her hair was tied at the back with a faded band. Things that she had owned since she was fourteen. Drawn to the worn-out and durable.

'Could we watch the film here?' she said.

'Not enough room.'

'I got an idea. Wait till I get dressed.'

He sat at the banquette until she came back. He was aware of her movement in the bedroom, the flexing in the alumin-ium frame of the caravan. When she was dressed she stood in front of a mirror propped up against coat hooks. He tried not to watch her. To be in her caravan while she showered, put on make-up. Grants of her person extended in the name of goodwill and what was practical. There were walking boots under the coat rack, fleeces, a yellow oilskin. She put on moisturiser and chapstick. This was the nature of things in her world, pared-down, dependable.

He put the projector and film into the box and followed her outside. The wind had got up. There was debris in the air, dead leaves, shoreline litter. The caravan rocked on its chassis. The door slapped against the side of the van.

'This way.' The caravan park lights shivered in the wind, the mounting poles flexing against their anchor lines. He followed her down a cement path behind the Lighthouse cafe to a concrete structure beyond the boundary of the light, the building set into a darkness that seemed to have been allowed for in its construction. Small dunes had formed against the seaward side of it.

'What is it?'

'They call it the Bomb Loft.'

She pulled back the bolt on the iron door at basement level, rust flakes falling from the hinge brackets. There were paint tins on the floor, faded signage from the caravan park and from the Lighthouse cafe, life belts put into storage for the winter. Water had gathered in depressions in the concrete flooring. They went up two flights of metal stairs, passing another steel door on the return. Unguarded lightbulbs hung from the ceiling and their shadows loomed in the high stair-well. They entered the top room by a door that had been sealed with black rubber, now rotted and hanging in strips.

'What class of place is this?' Cole said.

'They trained bomb aimers here.'

The room below them was floored with white canvas. A projector on the floor pointed downwards so that the trainee bomb aimer could lie on his stomach looking down on targets projected onto the canvas. Film of the Ruhr valley, the furnace buildings and steel mills. The navigator lay on the upper floor watching the lost cities reel past. Cologne. Dresden.

The projector body was bolted down. Acetates melded into the concrete. Corroded aluminium film spools on bent spindles lay against the wall. There was a smell of cellulose. Cole knelt to it. Brought the lens glass to his face, the iron sights convergent. He looked down into the room below. The canvas screening on the floor long since deteriorated, water-stained, torn where it had rotted, the only light on it that which came through the bomb aiming aperture on the floor of the room he was in.

'Let me see,' Kay said. She knelt on the floor beside him, her shoulder touching his.

'Look,' he said. There were footprints on the canvas, out-lined in black, one set smaller and facing the other, each printed footstep repeated from one corner of the canvas to the other.

'Dance steps,' she said. 'The man leads.'

'Who put them there?'

'Who knows?'

Cole rubbed his thumb along the names on the target plates. Railway marshalling yards, narrow estuary channels. The Pas-de-Calais. Targets and drop zones. One reel marked Pathfinder. Cole unspooled some of the film, the Pathfinder bombs in each frame flared in the darkness of the target zone. The film stock gone off, a chemical reek in the air.

'Cold in here,' Kay said. 'Feels like there's been no one in it for years.'

'They put their names here as well,' Cole said. The names of trainee bomb aimers etched into the matt blackout paint on the wall. She traced them with her finger. Jackson. Stepper. Jones.

'They sound like farm boys,' Cole said.

'Bet they wondered how they ended up here.'

'They wrote their names everywhere they went. The trees on the Avenue are covered. Usually got a girl's name there as well.'

The lost prairies empty of them now. Freckled girls in print dresses call their names but they are claimed in the black room.

'You thinking of using the wall?'

'No. There's a screen.'

She lowered the screen from a tripod bolted to the gable wall. The screen was frayed at the edges and there were rust marks and other staining on the waxed canvas.

'It'll do the job,' Cole said. He placed her projector onto an upturned crate and threaded the film onto the projector spool. Kay turned off the lights. The beginning of the film ran through the bulb housing, the first unexposed white frames marked with hairs, dust motes stuttering through the light. Letters started coming up then, fragments of names, lost captioning, the film stock degrading over the years in glyphs, lost text.

'The film is gone,' Kay said.

'Wait.' Shadows on the screen. Cole moved the focus wheel. The long dead ghosted into view.

'A dance,' Kay said.

It's a super eight film of a hop in a wartime dancehall. Early colour, a Cine-Kodak special. The first dances are the Shag Swing and the Lindy Hop. Some of the girls are wearing crinoline skirts with cotton half-slips belted at the waist, polka dot or plain silk tops. The dances are edge-of-reason jerky. The girls' red lipstick is pencilled-in. The look is heartless, lips pulled back from the teeth, eyes glittery. The men pull on cigarettes and watch the girls, eyes narrowed. A hungering. The camera pans across to a Negro soldier sitting at a table at the rear of the dance floor. Everything's moving too fast to see what's improvised and patched, the war-era fabrics, the darned hems, the stocking seams drawn on the calf. There's a hunger in the room, a carnal reckoning going on, and everyone knows there's a price to be paid. Outside the streets teem with servicemen and girls, and the best this night has to offer is a beach shelter with your skirt around your waist.

All of the dancers are white until the Negro comes out onto the floor. He's dancing with a young woman in a knee-length crinoline. The man moving her to the beat, bent at the waist, dreaming himself back to East Atlanta, Negro dance-halls beside the railway marshalling yard where the coloured girls are the right side of brazen, factory girl brass, all knowing looks and laughter. You can't tell if the girl he is dancing with knows that he is entangled in memory. Her hair is mar-celled and she is moving too fast to see her face, the film too old, the emulsions washed out, the colours bleeding.

Cole could hear the film coming off the spindle, the metal teeth mistimed on the disintegrating celluloid, the screen going blank as the film snapped. They waited in silence, the film end slapping against the projector housing as it turned, a silent jamboree of the dead at ten frames a second.

'What is that dance called?' Kay said.

'What?'

'The dance they were doing.'

'I don't know. I never danced in my life.'

'You serious?'

'What would I dance about?' He stood up. 'You can get the film spliced.'

'I used to dance.'

'When you weren't swimming.'

'I could teach you.' She danced to herself across the damp concrete, copying the steps they had seen on the film, marking time with her hand on her thigh. He could see that she knew the dance though not the steps. She knew the meaning.

'I don't think so. Not tonight anyhow. I better go.'

'I'll drive you back.'

'No. I'll walk.'

'She liked him.'

'Who?'

'The woman in the film. She liked that man she was dancing with. The black man.'

'More she liked everybody watching her dance with him.'

'Maybe.'

'A tease.' The girl was looking at the men, drawing it out of them, not liking her dancing with the black man. There was a howl gathering, something lone and craving at the back of the crowd.

'I'll go back to the caravan with you.'

'No call. There's no danger in this place.'

Cole looked around the loft, the dismantled crafts of war, the cylinders carrying the contours of the century's ruin, the record of war degrading in its own spoil. Hers a pale refugee face in this destitute acreage.

'Thanks for the projector. I have to go see Lily anyway.'

*

Lily was awake when Kay went to the house on the Limekiln road.

'I see you. From top window.'

'Seen what Lily?'

'Going up to the Bomb Loft I seen you. Not to go to that Bomb Loft.'

'We had a film show.'

'What film?'

'Something I found in a second-hand shop.'

'With man?'

'Why would you think that, Lily?'

'Come in swing hips like that, missy, there's a man.'

'I don't think so, Lily.'

'You man eyes on you.'

'I don't have man eyes, whatever those are. I have no luck with the men.'

'That not stop you.'

'Stopped me before now.'

'Something not right about you tonight, girl.'

'Why's that, Lily?'

'The black thing is different. Behind you. I don't mind the name.'

'My shadow.'

'Shadow. Different to shadow last night. You seen film?'

'Wasn't a proper film. A home movie like.'

'Home movie what?'

'People dancing.'

'Did you ever see a hare dance? Up on two hind legs in the moonlight and dance.'

'I never did, Lily. Are your night-time tablets taken?'

'I did took them, Kay.'

'Good woman. Now up them stairs.'

Lily got to her feet. She didn't like to be helped. She got cross if you reached out a hand. People were always reaching out to pluck things from her. Her peace of mind, her memories. So much was already gone. In cotton nightdress and slippers she crossed the cold tile floor.

'I don't sound me,' she said, 'the feet.'

'You're as light as a feather, Lil.'

'Me's as light as the dust,' she said, and went up the stairs like something scattered by the wind. Kay heard the bedroom door close. She turned off the main light. She stood in the hallway at the bottom of the stairs to put on her coat when light fell on her from above. Lily was standing at the head of the stairs, her nightdress and hair lit from behind by the landing light.

'Remember me things. Can't say.'

'What do you remember, Lil?'

'My name.'

'Lily?'

'Not always. Name change.'

'Who changed your name?'

'Me's as light as a feather. Me's as light as the dust.' And Lily was gone.

*

Cole got back to the hotel after midnight. Sleet had gathered in the shadowed corners of the Hollow. He rang the bell and the door was answered by the pale girl who had been with the Brethren at the harbour. She handed his key across the desk. Her nails were cut short and unvarnished. She did not wear any make-up. The reception seemed more austere for her being there, her blue eyes looking past him to an unadorned truth, the threadbare carpets and yellowed ceilings taking on the attributes of a meeting house, a place where dissenters gathered, men of God, fearful, harried, bent to their tracts.

'I haven't seen you here before.'

'I work nights.'

'The hotel is quiet.'

'It is always quiet.'

'Against the law to chat to guests?'

'There is no such rule. I have work to do, if you don't mind.' When she moved he saw there was a bruise on her collarbone. She pulled the collar of her shirt across to conceal it and he looked away. Hurt had its laws too. He knew them.

His room was on the third storey at the rear of the hotel. He went along ill-lit passages, the carpet giving way to unpolished floorboards, the paintwork notched and chipped, feeling cold air on his face from the window sashes. There were white-tiled toilets along the corridors, the tiling stained green where it touched copper piping. He went into the toilet on his landing. The cistern ran steadily into the chipped bowl. The windowpane above the cistern was broken and sleet made a small heap on the windowsill, fine crystalline particles like the icy siftings of the starlit night sky. He thought he heard footsteps passing on the corridor outside, something barefoot and furtive, stealthy on the move. He had seen no other guest on this floor. He went to the door and listened but there was no sound now in the corridor. He waited. People had their reasons to be abroad at this hour, to avail themselves of night's parole.

He unlocked his room and closed the door. The iron radiators had been shut off since dusk and his breath clouded in front of him. The room was in the eaves, the ceiling angled above the bed in tongue and groove planking. He turned on the radio and listened to the weather forecast. Arctic air masses flowing down from the north, warnings about blizzard conditions, the mountain and coastal routes to the east of the town under threat of closure.

He looked for the photograph he had left on the bedside locker. The two boys. The photograph had been torn in two and placed on the pillow, one half missing. He picked it up. The paper had been ripped down the middle and the younger boy removed.

The radio spoke of days of cold weather. Cole went to the window and leaned his head against the glass. He could see the outline of the hospital on the hill, risen above the town like a gaunt moonlit cathedral, a place of old hauntings, monkish reverence, cowled figures moving in ruined cloisters. Vows observed, penance undertaken.

He held the torn photograph in his palm and the warmth of his skin softened the lacquer. He smoothed it and put it in his wallet.

Seven

Morne
23rd November 2000

Magistrate Isaac Corry's house stood at the start of the Parade, an unlit annexe on the high ground above the harbour with a promenade of three-storey houses on both sides leaning in on each other. A once fashionable street now gone to ruin. The Magistrate's name and occupation in unpolished brass plate on the door. A Mason's dividers etched in plaster above the adjacent house but the Masons no longer held their ceremonies there. Across the street the lead roof fittings of two buildings had been stripped and sold so that the roofs collapsed inwards. Upritchard, as he followed Lynch, looked up to see the night sky through the upper-storey windows, each holding what looked like a bright, single constellation. Once windows, he thought, but star-frames now.

Corry let them in to the downstairs office. The office was cold and ill-lit. Cardboard-bound client files were massed on the floor and on the desk. Books on equity and land law in a glass case. A frosted glass divider bore the name Isaac Corry in gilt lettering. Corry sat down at the desk and lit a cigarette. He was grey-faced, elderly, an apostle of bad faith.

'You're here about the new man in the town,' Corry said.

People brought information to the Magistrate. Lynch had seen it through the court years. Tipstaffs whispered to him. Doormen and court stenographers leaned towards him confidentially. People felt the need to unburden themselves.

'Says he's an MOD solicitor.'

'The land the body was found on. Ministry of Defence.'

'As well as the land where the sandpit is. This is on my head. They're after me.'

'People don't give a damn about your patch of sand, Wesley.'

'I hear you have a proposed prosecution in relation to the disposal of unauthorised waste at Pirnmill.'

'Suddenly it's my prosecution.'

'To the disposal of waste products.'

'They weren't disposed of. They were dumped. The waste wasn't products. It was needles, toxins, chemicals, soiled sanitary products, laboratory effluent. But there is insufficient evidence to hold out a reasonable prospect of a successful prosecution.'

'You won't convict me?'

'As always, Wesley.'

'You're ancient, Upritchard,' Lynch said. 'Nobody's going to send you to prison for this kind of thing anyway.'

'Never mind that,' Corry said. 'His name is Cole?'

'Yes.'

'From where?'

'Scotland, he says.'

'There's a problem.'

'There's always a problem.'

'According to the Ministry there is no solicitor by the name of Cole working for the MOD, or contracted to them.'

'So he is an interloper. A sneak.'

'Who knows who he is?'

'A ghost,' Upritchard said.

'Be quiet, Wesley.'

'Somebody must have heard of him,' Lynch said. 'I'll contact Strathclyde police.'

'Good. What has he been doing?'

'Measuring the ground at the dump pit. Checking land maps in the library.'

'He's looking for more than land maps in the library,' the Magistrate said.

'I'll speak my piece,' Upritchard said.

'Then speak it,' the Magistrate said.

'I told you then and I'm telling you now. The whole lot should have been burned. Every deed, every police record, every scrap of paper on everything we ever did.'

'Records are kept. Records protect.'

'Protect against who?'

'Against people like us.'

'Do you have them here, Isaac?'

'If I did I wouldn't tell you. Did you keep any records from your days as Superintendent of the home?'

'If I did I wouldn't tell anyone either.'

'That means you have something.'

'Never mind the records, what about the body?' Lynch said. 'It could be record enough as it is. We can't hold the autopsy off for ever. What is there to lose from doing it?'

'Cause of death would be hard to ascertain after so much time has passed.'

'It isn't how she died that has me lying awake at night,'

Lynch said, 'but who she is.'

'How would anyone find that out? There are no traces of her existence.'

'Dental records. We didn't take the dental records.'

'Where are the dental records kept?'

'Surgery in the home.'

'What about the autopsy?'

'Ask Corry here. He's the coroner.'

'Under the Coroners Act I may order an autopsy or I may not. In any case I will describe it as being of limited use due to chemical contamination of the corpse.'

'There's your way out.'

'There'll be a hearing in the coroner's court on Tuesday. Weather permitting. Lynch will give evidence pertaining to the finding of the body during sand quarrying.'

The town had its secrets and they were its stewards.

'Better if she had never been found,' Lynch said.

'Better if she had never been born, but we didn't get the choosing of that, did we?'

Corry watched Lynch and Upritchard from the upstairs window as they walked back towards the centre of town. A single streetlight made their shadows stretch out in front of them under the ruined facades of the grand houses. The starlight streamed through the empty window frames. As though the merchant dead held court in their rooms of collapsed stucco, the sprung maple dance floors rotted, fireplaces long ripped out and sold, the bloodless heirs dead.

He put coal on the study fire and went to the roll-top desk. His lawyer's wig in its tin canister, his frayed black robe on its hanger. A photograph of his wife stood on top of the desk. She was wearing a long dress in white silk gathered at the waist. She was a tall woman, hollow-cheeked, growing into her gauntness, inhabiting the deep sunken eyes, heiress to the shadows. Older than him. From the start she would not let him touch her in the house. She had liked to dance and he had driven her to dances through the post-war decades, led her through the dance steps in forgotten provincial hotels and ballrooms. The Great Northern. The Maritime. On the way home she directed him to the forgotten spaces, laybys, old pierhead buildings now derelict, the forecourts of old country mansions, the houses of lost desire.

He recalled her in the back seat of the car directing his hand to the top of her dress. He recalled her on the bonnet of the car on the side of the Limekiln road, her skirt raised, the curlews and the night wind in the light gantries offshore giving voice to the night. He remembered her in the roof-less drawing room of a fallen mansion. Afterwards he had walked to the dry fountain on the ruined lawns, the lime-stone surround cracked and stained. She had called after him in a hoarse voice. She was not done with her ravening, she was not sated in the houses of the dead. There were covenants with them still to be observed.

He reached into the back of the desk for the letters. He wondered why he had kept them there and why he had not locked them in the strong room. He put them in his pocket. They would be put under lock and key that night.

Rebecca had found the letters the night she left him. She had opened them out on the desk and was reading them when he came in from court.

'Dear Christ that I allowed myself to be any part of you and your friends.'

'You did not allow it. Your father ordered it.'

'More fool me that I didn't throw myself in the tide sooner than allow you to lay a hand on me.' She rose and left the room. When he got up the next morning she had gone. Now the letters were gone as well.

*

Letter #1

Remember about the aerodrome beside the sea and our hut there's a sandpit full of water I let on it's a lagoon with the silvery moon shining on it there's a bottle of Smirnoff there for me and you haha. You can see the lights of the ships beyond the bar waiting for the tide waiting waiting. They're going everywhere all over the world. Singapore! Malaysia! I seen a lorry going past with Buenos Aires wrote on the side of it where they do the tango. I'd do the tango with you and click my fingers if you were here you could tango me again and again.

Would you believe it think of all the places we could go me and you lovers on a shore. Upritchard was staring again today he never laid a finger on me but I felt his eyes on me when I went past he says he was happy to get shut of you out of the place I says to myself don't be so glad Mr Creep you got the crazy girl you better believe it. He says his heart is broke with me he wouldn't know a broken heart if one fell on him. I'll put manners on you he says he doesn't know what manners is.

If it's a boy I'll call it after you a girl I don't know.

Love love love Reay xxxxxxxx

Eight

Pirnmill Aerodrome
1st September 1944

'What are you good at, Hooper?'

'I don't know, Sir.'

'He doesn't know. What did you do in whatever backwoods you was brought up in?'

'Key Road, East Atlanta, Sergeant. Worked the allotments, Sir.'

'Worked the allotments. You see any okra around here? Collard greens?'

'No, Sergeant Evans.'

'You're straight off the plane and wet around the ears, isn't that right?'

'Yes, Sergeant.'

'I could put you to latrines.'

'I worked the movie theatre, Sir, for Mr Benson.'

'A Negro movie house, is that it?'

'Yes, Sir. I helped in the projector room.' Carrying the reels up the stairs for the projectionist, Benson too fat to do it himself. The tin-roof theatre hot in the summer, cold in the winter. Watching Benson thread the film through the lens, adjust the knurled focus knob.

'I could put you to sweep floors in the Bomb Loft.'

'Sarge.'

'Can you work the projector?'

'Yes, Sergeant.'

'What's the danger associated with nitrate film?'

'It burns.'

'What happens if you put it in water?'

'Keeps burning.'

'What's a cue mark?'

'Tells you when a reel is about to end, Sergeant.'

'Reckon you do know what you're talking about. You got the job. Burn no film. Keep the gate clean. You know you're the only Negro left on this base?'

'Am I, Sarge?'

'You got Niggertown to yourself. There's them would rather not have you here. There's them would put a rope over a tree branch. Keep your eyes peeled is what I'm saying.'

Nine

Morne Children's Home
July 1972

Her real name was not Reay but she called herself that. Harper thought it was because the word sounded like sunlight but she said it reminded her of girls in other places who had lives of downbeat glamour in coffee bars, girls in slacks who narrowed their eyes and blew smoke at strange men in suits in places like London and places like the pier in the Point. She could be one of them. A girl who would not admit to longings but would look moody out of windows and ignore the stares of men. There would be urban settings. Tarmac roads slick with rain at dawn. There would be unspoken looks. They would know what it was like to be young and doomed.

She had a city girl look about her. She wore cheesecloth shirts and oxblood Doc Martens. You imagined her in monochrome riot footage. Football hooligans in post-industrial landscapes. Guileful boys with feather cuts. Girls in parallels striking poses in city waste grounds. Angels cast down from forbidden heavens of their own imagining.

Harper dreamed the same dreams as Reay. We'll run away, me and you, he said, and be an outlaw couple. We'll sleep in cars and wake in the pale dawn. Harper liked the same places as her. They would walk down the bank to the workhouse graveyard. She wanted him to talk about his dreams but he had none, he said.

'We'll have to stop somewhere,' she said, 'we can't run for the rest of our lives.'

'We'll stop at the Black Laws,' he said.

'Where's that?'

'It's in Lanarkshire. Where me and Ghost came from.'

'Scotland? What's there?'

'At the Black Laws? Hills. Little hills and the stars.'

'I'm not really a hills and stars girl. I'm more of a bright lights girl.'

'We'll use the Black Laws as a base.'

'What about the boy? We can't go without our ghost.'

'I'm not leaving him here. Me and him got sent here together.'

'Then what are we going to do?'

'We come back for him. I'm not leaving him.'

'I never asked you to.'

'Not with the Superintendent.'

'It's not just him.'

'But he's the worst. We could go to the Magistrate about him.'

'The Magistrate's no good to us.'

'We could go to the Matron.'

'I don't know if I trust her. She's married to the bastard Magistrate.'

'No love lost between them too, as far as I can see. They say she done something bad and her da was a preacher and he gave her to him.'

'You can't give somebody away.'

'You can if you're part of them Brethren.'

Harper had put two pallets together and spread a blanket over them. He was at home with the disused and the worn-out. Old fishermen's huts and derelict barns. Places worked into the landscape and barely seen. He furnished them with armchairs dumped on the shore, made tables from fish boxes and beds from pallets dragged from the tide. It was Harper who found the Nissen hut at the edge of the aerodrome. It was an expertise he had, finding things, putting things together.

They brought Cole with them sometimes. Reay called him Ghost. She said you'd hardly know he was about. She said it was like he was made of air. Harper and Reay on a pallet bed under a pile of coats, the shiftings and whispery manoeuvres under the blankets, the small muffled sounds she made, the soft impacted phonetics, teenagers trying to hide it, half-formed phrases of an old language. The boy would move to a window or sit in the doorway looking out, clouds gathering on the horizon.

Afterwards they'd sit round a table Harper had made, acting out whatever facsimile of home they could gather between them. Reay putting out slices of bread on the table, Harper looking down on them, some stern idea of fatherhood in his stance. None of them knowing how it was done, just that there were other fatherhoods out there that had to be kept at bay. Standing in doorways swaying, red-eyed. Fathers with fists. Fathers with belts. Harper making the boy say please and thank you, trying out the words in his mouth like everything else in the hut salvaged from other people's lives. Warning the boy. Stay away from Upritchard. Be a ghost when he was around, him and his pals. They were always writing reports. They had Reay's card marked, she said, and he didn't want to get caught up in it.

*

Confidential

Report of Guardian ad Litem for Karen Wilkinson (also known as Reay Wilkinson)

The inmate was described as being disruptive. On several occasions she left the premises at night by forcing doors or windows and was returned by local constabulary. Her mother is described as being both depressive and alcoholic. No father is listed on her birth certificate. It appeared that she was highly sexualised. Staff reported instances of inappropriate behaviour. Staff member A stated that 'I felt as if she was trying to seduce me.' At the request of the Superintendent, Dr Eugene examined her to ascertain if she was 'virgo intacta'. He described the attempted examination as being 'most unpleasant' and that it was accompanied by 'lewd and suggestive' remarks from Miss Wilkinson. He was unable to establish if the inmate had indulged in carnal relations due to the violence of her reaction. Restraint was proposed but it was suggested that it might be counter-productive. It would seem that she had established relationships with several of the male inmates despite segregation and is thought to have been a negative influence. The Superintendent seemed confident that disciplinary measures would be effective.

Given this day, 10th July 1972

Isaac Corry RM

Ten

Morne
24th November 2000

Cole walked up Hospital Street and tried the police station intercom. There was no reply. The wall beneath the intercom was black with verdigris running through it. There was a noticeboard on the station wall. Pinboard covered in abraded Perspex, condensation on the inside so that you could barely pick out words on the yellowed handbills and posters pinned up inside, old warnings about shoplifters, penalties for drink drivers, the malefactors of another era, their sins long since paid for. Over the town rooftops he could see snow blowing in from the sea, pale, unnavigable squalls yet to make landfall.

He walked back to the bottom of the hill. There was an arcade leading off to the right, the shopfronts empty except for a florist's. He entered and waited at the counter. A woman came out from the back, wiping her hands on her jeans.

'The lorry hasn't come. The ferry's held up with the weather. I got no tulips or chrysanthemums. Nothing like that.'

'I don't need anything fancy,' he said.

'You're in the right place for nothing fancy. I do more funerals than weddings and not that many of them. What are you in for?'

'Any weddings coming up?'

'No. Is there a lady in view?'

'No lady. Not among the living anyhow.'

'Was I meant to laugh there?'

'No.'

'Good. It kind of caught in my throat. What do you want?'

'Roses.'

'I always got roses. Six do you?'

'Yes. What are those for?'

'Flowers for the meeting house. Lilies. Them I grow in the hothouse.'

The scent of the flowers reached Cole. There was a memory of a pot broken on a wooden floor and a smell of lilies.

'You seen a ghost, Mister?'

'I never liked the smell of them.'

'Me neither. The last minister always had them and they kept it up.'

'The last one?'

'The Reverend Davidson. He lived to a great age.'

'Upritchard is there now.'

'He's no more a reverend than you and me. Him and his friends ran the town into the ground since they were young.'

'The Brethren?'

'There's more than one Brethren afoot in this place. Take your flowers, Mister.'

Cole walked across the square to the foot of the Meeting House road, along the back wall of the hospital to the meeting house graveyard, a pristine and desolate acre of polished headstones. He stepped down the hill towards the river where the forgotten lay, the graves unweeded. Yew trees had grown up through the graves and the roots had buckled the earth, the stone surrounds broken in places and lifted clear of the cracked cement capping, the headstones off-centre. Resurrection had failed them. Faded artificial flowers still remained on some graves, perpetual flames in plastic containers long since gone out. In the thorn trees at the river supplicants had tied torn pieces of clothing to the branches. Headscarves, shoelaces, nylon tights, strips torn from underwear, silken, transgressive, lewd. In the crevices of the trees they had placed coins, candles, hair tied up with thread, a child's toy car, candle stubs.

Cole made his way through the thorn trees, the occult landscape. He came out at the top of the slope and crossed to the morgue steps, unseen by Lynch's cameras. He placed the roses on the steps of the morgue.

The Chalets, Limekiln Road

Lily stick paper with name to things to remember. Name kettle. Name sink. Name fridge. When Lily's back door was opened all the notes she had written moved in the draught then stopped. Sound of something took to flight in her room. Ink faded away on some notes so you not see what was wrote on them but she kept them up for there once were names for all things and might be again.

'Get very cold,' she told Kay. 'Freeze you in caravan.'

'Not much warmer in the chalet, Lily.'

'Get so cold. What your name?'

'Kay, Lily, I told you so many times.'

Before dark the branches of the alder trees on the shore glittered with rime. There were lapwings on the bents driven from the continent to look for food. The signs Lily knew forever. Stunted growing in the dark earth, buds and leaf tips like burned things. Hoar ice in the machair channels. Found a black beetle froze in a puddle. White moth froze to branch.

That morning Lily had taken herself to the outhouse. There was a toilet and newspaper on a nail beside it. There was new blood on the cistern and the toilet bowl. There was blood smeared on the tongue and groove walls. There were creosote smells, unclean balms. The cistern ran.

Lily had not heard the killing but her mother had told her that birds did not make any noise when they were taken in the air.

She searched the bents until she found a dead sparrow-hawk. It had been shot, what mandate of flight it had possessed now rendered up to some court of the air. She brought it down to the house. She drove a nail into the outhouse wall and looped wire around the bird and left it gibbeted there. She looked at the dark carrion meat under the feathers and the yellow talons. She pushed the pin feathers away from the eyes so that they could see.

'Why did you nail a dead bird to the outhouse, Lily?' Kay said.

'Hawk died a thrush in outhouse. Fly it through window hungry thing.'

'A hawk killed a thrush in the outhouse?'

'Hawk hungry. Hawk died it.'

'What's a dead bird on the door going to do?'

'Fright her other hawk birds. Them not come near out-house.'

'They won't come near the dead hawk, is that it?'

'Scare them.'

'You might be right.'

'Scare them. Scare me too.' The sparrowhawk's body a feathered husk turning in the night wind. Shotgun pellets rattled in the ribcage. The yellow fire in the raptor eye was gone. The cornea turned brown but the black slit iris was still there, forever alert as though a fierce guard remained, some old fastness of the air held.

Kay went to the pool before work. She wore her swimming costume under a spandex jacket. She liked breathable fabrics, Gore-Tex, clothing that was well-used and proven. There was a climbing wall in the high school gym that she had used in the summer. She liked the nubbed holds of the climbing wall, the thought-out geometries and overhangs. Mountains were for the dauntless, bearded Victorians in crampons. The pool a post-war lido built out into the sea, tide-filled. A trawler had slipped her moorings and been driven against the ocean side of the pool during an easterly years ago and rested there, beyond salvage, the bows stoved in against the concrete. At high tide only the mastheads and wheelhouse antennae were visible above the water. The VHF array bearing hanks of weed, which streamed in the east wind like the pennants of the drowned. Her nameplate and registration still on the bow, the Brighter Morn.

The tide was high and the water had risen as far as the entrance to the cubicles. Things of the sea scuttling under the benches. She stood at the entrance kiosk for a moment, watching trawlers go out. The water smoked at the prows as they inched round the pierhead, a frozen mist covering the sound of the engines, the boats drifting out to sea, wheelhouse and superstructure hidden by the cold mist, seeming like floating hulks, unmanned. Ghost boats. Fog tendrils wreathed through the iron handrails on the edge of the pool, sub-zero emanations, and sank to the surface of the pool water. She took off her jacket and folded it at the edge of the water, her swimsuit svelte, snugly contoured, making her feel part of a higher purpose. Early light on the icy cupola domes above the low mist, on the broken mouldings, the rust streaks on the walls, the frozen palaces of the north. She got into the water and swam in silence.

She dressed at the edge of the pool. She took off her swimsuit and towelled herself down. She had forgotten her swim cap and she wrapped the towel around her wet hair as she reached for her clothes. No one could have seen her in the fog. The derelict baths like the frozen palaces of the north and she was the ice princess, pale, nude, regal. Her phone rang.

'Miss Chambers?'

'Yes.'

'Sergeant Lynch. There's been a break-in at the library.'

On the way from the harbour the radio reported dangerous driving conditions in the hinterland, black ice on minor roads, warnings of snow to come, accumulations on high ground. The signal seemed to be coming from some distant province. People's voices kept fading. There was persistent static.

*

The blue light of the building alarm flashed through the frozen fog, Lynch barely visible at the top of the library stairs until he moved, his figure distorted in the mist. Scenes from an eerie fiction. Swirling mist, looming figures.

'I examined the outside of the building,' Lynch said. He showed her where the old putty on a side window had been picked away, the small pane removed.

'They got in easy. All they had to do was reach in to the catch.'

Kay unlocked the front door. Thinking about scenes of ransack, images of violated interiors, contents strewn, drawers rifled. She didn't expect the library to be intact. She looked through the front desk. Walked the bookshelves.

'They took nothing.'

'You sure?'

'There's nothing to steal.'

'No cash. Fines or that sort of thing?'

'No.'

'Sometimes that happens. They get disturbed and leave. Sometimes they just like to do it. They get into someone's house and watch the TV, eat something from the fridge.'

'Bravado.'

'Something like that. They didn't leave much to go on. I'll file a report.'

'OK.'

'You need to do something about your security. Check the caravan locks. Fit an alarm.'

'You think I need to?'

'There's some strange characters about. Better safe than sorry.'

'Where are the police when you need them?'

'I'm the police for now. The others have to travel here. The weather gets any worse the road will be closed. We have to look after ourselves here. Always did.'

'The body you found.'

'What about it?'

'Is it still up in the hospital?'

'Where else would it be?'

'When will the inquest be held?'

'It's been adjourned.'

'Why?'

'We're waiting for them to send someone to perform an autopsy. Magistrate wants the autopsy and inquest to be held in the town. Important to him they don't close the court. Transfer its functions.'

'Will someone come soon?'

'Not in this weather.'

'She shouldn't be lying up there on her own.'

'She can lie there until the resurrection. That body didn't burgle the library. Means nothing to nobody around here. Sort out your security. I've better things to be doing.'

When Lynch left she walked around the library. It would have been better if something had been taken. She would have been able to picture petty criminals, disgruntled youths. A few hours ago someone had been here. They had left a silence behind. She thought of a lone figure breathing in the dark, walking the long institutional corridors. She imagined stealthy footsteps, a pale, motiveless stare. She wondered who had been watching her at the swimming baths. She wondered if it was the same person.

She went down to the basement. The heating was off and the basement was cold. The storage room had taken on the look of a crime scene. Old boots, crumpled tunics, forage caps left in a corner. It looked ransacked under the yellow, unshaded light. She thought of men walking in line, standing behind barbed wire. There was a brown envelope pinned to the front of the uniform given to her by Mrs Orr.

She looked up. Cole stood on the gantry looking down at her.

'What are you doing up there?'

'The door was open.'

'You have to get permission to come down here.'

'There was no one at the desk to ask. What's wrong?'

'We got broken into.'

'I saw the squad car. Anything taken?'

'No.'

'Lucky.'

'Something was left.' She held up the brown envelope.

'What is it?'

She opened the envelope. Two sheets of utility paper, yellowed and brittle.

'Court documents.'

'You can tell from there?'

'They always look the same. They always smell the same.'

'He frightened me.'

'Who?'

'Lynch. I don't know why I'm telling you this.'

'You haven't told me anything.'

'He said to check the security on my caravan.'

'Not a bad idea.'

'He said there were people out there.'

'Those kind of people are always out there.'

'Why do you say that?'

'Because they are.'

'You could be one of them. Those kind of people.' His shadow cast on the wall behind him by the flat yellow light. She felt alone, open to dread. People of shadowy authority standing over her.

'I could be.'

'Sorry.'

'You're right to be careful. You want me to come out? Put a stronger lock in the door. Check the windows.'

'I don't need favours. Couldn't live like that. I like my place the way it is. I'm going to take this upstairs and look at it.'

'Can I look at the records again?'

'I'm off my high horse. I'm sorry, I was frightened. Did you lock the room after you?'

'No.'

'Check your own stuff before you check my caravan.'

He took off his overcoat, folded it and put in on top of a filing cabinet. He was wearing a grey suit and open-neck white shirt.

'Like Bletchley Park down here,' she said.

'Where's Bletchley Park?'

'It's where they broke the German codes during the war. The Enigma machine.' She had seen photographs of people in windowless rooms, men wearing glasses with heavy frames, pale, strained faces searching for encryption keys, the dense spaced numerals.

'Could do with an Enigma machine to work out what's happening with this inquest.'

'An inquest is an inquest.'

'They can drag on for years. Nobody is in any hurry with this one.'

The room downstairs looked the way it had when he left. The dented filing cabinets were not locked. The files he had taken out were on the table or stacked on the floor beside. His notebook was in the middle of the table, two pens lined up beside it.

'Are you all right?'

'The caravan was always safe,' she said. 'I sit out in the summertime when the nights are warm. I leave the door open.'

Summer nights. It was starting to feel as if they had never happened. Half-drunk in flip-flops. The feel of flimsy outdoor furniture, the feel of sun-bleached fabric under your thighs. Teenage voices carrying from the sand dunes, a radio playing from an open caravan door, a couple walking home talking in low voices. Late-summer reveries. Upstairs she opened the envelope and took out the documents.

Statement of Facts re events of 9th December 1944 as presented to the Court Martial of Private Gabriel Hooper

Private Gabriel Hooper of Company D 390th Engineer Regiment stationed at Pirnmill Airbase went on proper pass to the nearby town of Warrenpoint on the evening of 9th December 1944. He visited several public houses and a dance held at the Women's Institute hall. Having missed the lorry that was to bring servicemen from the dancehall to the airbase at Pirnmill, it is alleged he fell into the company of Elspeth Davidson, a local girl of sixteen years. Miss Davidson's father has made a deposition on her behalf. In his deposition he states that his daughter attended the social club in Warrenpoint as part of a charity drive to provide teas and light refreshments to the American soldiers. After the dance refreshments were served, then Miss Davidson set out to walk back to her home. Her father states that she had become detached from her missionary companion but she must have decided to continue on alone. There had been a fall of snow that evening and while it was dark there was a certain degree of luminosity.

Private Hooper states that he left the vicinity of the Women's Institute hall at 00.30 and walked in the direction of Pirnmill Airbase. It is Private Hooper's contention that Miss Davidson met him on the road and accompanied him. He maintains that Miss Davidson had danced with him earlier that evening. Miss Davidson's father's deposition maintains that she had seen him at several social events prior to the evening in question and had told her father that she 'felt sorry' for him as he was the only soldier of colour present. There were no other soldiers on the road that night. There was a truck going back to the camp but the defendant maintains that the truck drove off without him, the occupants telling the driver to 'drive on, let the black bastard walk'. There were few people walking that night and therefore no witnesses to attest to the veracity of the defendant's account.

The defendant maintains that Miss Davidson accompanied him back to the Bomb Loft, which was the bomb aiming practice range where he worked as a projection assistant. There were no witnesses to their entrance or egress from the Bomb Loft which is to the seaward side of the airfield complex, nor is there any physical evidence, although Sergeant Evans, the senior NCO in charge of the Bomb Loft, asserts that there were footprints on the canvas flooring of the projection room and that there had been no such footprints on the flooring when he left the loft at approximately 18.30 on the previous evening.

The complainant's affidavit states that the defendant then offered to accompany Miss Davidson to her home close to the Meeting House road gospel hall and that the defendant suggested a short cut via the Avenue, which skirts the back of the hospital and is a short cut by day and a popular location for courting couples at night. The affidavit states that in retrospect it seemed that the accused had hatched a plan but was prevented from carrying it out by the presence of other couples in the Avenue area that night.

The accused further states that they made an arrangement to meet later in the week to attend a movie in the local movie theatre or picture house. All we know of Miss Davidson's side of the matter is presented by way of affidavit from her father, the said affidavit refuting anything of the kind. The affidavit states that Miss Davidson did not attend the film that night or any other night since it would be in contravention of her religious principles, which strictly forbade such entertainments.

It is the prosecution's contention, again by way of affidavit from Miss Davidson's father, that the accused lay in wait for Miss Davidson on the night of the attack at a point halfway along the location known locally as the Avenue, a secluded tree-lined drive. There he accosted her violently with the results that we now know of. The defence seems to rest entirely on the accused's alleged visit to the cinema with Miss Davidson and the assertion that their acquaintance was at all times consensual. He further states that he left Miss Davidson outside the movie theatre and proceeded home to his quarters at the airbase. There is of course no evidence of the defendant entering the gates of the airbase that night as he, in his own words, 'went in and out under the wire'. There are no witnesses to his coming and going since, as the only coloured person on the site, he had sole use of the quarters dedicated to coloured servicemen.

Eleven

Morne Old People's Home
24th November 2000

Corry parked outside the old people's quarters at the hospital. He entered the Nissen huts by the back door. The front door opened onto a windowless dayroom. Light came from iron-framed skylights set into the ceiling vault. Five corridors led to wards, with a glassed-in inspection room to the right of the main doorway. The residents were grouped at the centre of the room. One raised her hand at him slowly as though in the habit of command. A hairless old man held the room in an unblinking stare. Gaunt peers and courtesans.

There were roses in a porcelain vase on the sideboard and he wondered who would bring such blooms to this strange court. He asked a nurse to direct him and she sent him along the middle corridor. He wore an overcoat and scarf but he no longer felt the cold. The corridor was deserted. He glimpsed the bedridden through open doors. White hair, sunken faces, wraiths adrift in the airy realms of forgetting. Eugene's door was closed. He went in without knocking. Eugene still a large man with hair sprouting from his pyjama cuffs. Eugene had said that he was Hungarian. From the Carpathians or some other remote and mountainous province. The first time Corry saw him Eugene had been carrying a suitcase bound with a belt and a leather case of instruments.

'Cold out there.' Corry sat down on the edge of the bed. 'Freezing.' Eugene did not look at him. He had not spoken for years.

'They found a body. At the sandpit. A girl.' Eugene did not reply and Corry did not expect him to. It was the silence of some durance, honed and knowing. They had never proved dementia. There was nothing absent in Eugene's demeanour. Corry thought about some old religion, cabalistic in nature. Men in skullcaps rocking on their heels, working their way into the profane mysteries.

'Twenty-eight years ago, Eugene. Things we did not speak about. Now there is a need to know.'

Corry got up and went to the window. There was a framed photograph on the sill. Unsmiling men and women in the dress of long ago. They looked respectable, a European bour-geoisie between the wars. The men in hats and moustaches, women in crinolines. Sombre with the burdens of forgotten worlds.

'I might as well be talking to the wall.'

An orderly came into the room, a girl in her early twenties carrying a tray. Blonde hair, a country face, wind-chapped. Corry had seen her at the Brethren meeting house.

'I'm sorry, Mr Corry. I was to feed him. I can come back.'

'No. Please. We can't starve the man.'

'Routine is very important.' She put the tray down on a side table.

'Of course.'

'He's had disruption enough.'

'What class of disruption would that be?'

'He got out one night. Run away so he did.'

'Careless.'

'I think somebody let him out. The doors are locked.'

'One night?'

'What do you mean?'

'Did he only get out one night?'

'I don't know. He doesn't look fit to go nowhere. Found him at the aerodrome so they did.'

'Has anyone been to see him apart from me?'

'I don't know.'

'You don't know?'

'I heard voices from the room.'

'You didn't look?'

'There was nothing in the day book.'

'Who was it?'

'Nobody.'

'Don't lie to me.'

'I think it was your wife, Mr Corry.'

Twelve

Shepton Mallet
20th January 1945

Hooper wondered what would happen if Lindbergh was being court martialled in a week's time, what he'd do. Hands in pockets, speaking in a slow drawl, setting things out for the judges the way they were. Hooper saw him wearing a leather flying jacket edged with sheepskin, an air force forage cap. There'd be a long-distance stare, a prairie man's gift for unhurried appraisal. Captain Phair talked of affidavits and rebuttals. Lawyer talk that Hooper knew wouldn't sway any white court that was trying a black man.

Hooper stood at the cell windows every night looking at the sky. He could hear the planes overhead, the thrumming squadrons flying in deep formation towards the target zones. The skies over Berlin. The inky skies over Dresden. What you saw between the flak bursts, the controls bucking in your hands, bank and rudder. Feeling the updraught, the yaw and pitch, the altimeter at 20,000 feet, fathoms of air beneath the wings.

Lindbergh would let the court know how it was. The way that things happen unknown to yourself. Lindbergh would say the name Elspeth out loud and not be ashamed. He would tell how they met in a clear voice.

Morne
9th December 1944

The truck back to the camp was due to leave Warrenpoint at twelve. Hooper came out of the dance and walked towards the meeting place, the square in blackout. You could hear ships in the dark, the fender-slip against the quay, the keel noises, the chop of the water between hull and pier. He could hear curlews in the shallows at the far side of the lough, the piped-out marsh reveille lonesome after the warmth and noise of the dance. A truck engine started and he heard men's booted feet making towards it though you could not see them. He could make out the canvas awning of the truck and he ran towards it, the tailgate down, lit cigarettes in the dark, men's voices. A man banged on the truck cab.

'Let the black bastard walk.'

'Drive on.'

'Go on. Drive.'

He stood in the square watching the truck diminish, its exhaust hanging in a blue line across the open space, changing up gears at the shoreline. He'd miss curfew but he could get in under the wire.

'Hello.'

The girl he had danced with was standing under a shop awning. She was wearing a pale knee-length coat and white gloves.

'Are you on your own?'

'I came with my girlfriend, Margaret.'

'Where is she?'

'She is with her young man. Over there. He's a pilot. She's

very mysterious about him. It's his last week before he goes overseas.'

A young woman and a man wearing a forage cap stood together under a shop awning further down the street, her head against his shoulder, her voice carrying but not the words, murmurings of parting repeated all over Europe.

'There's a Pathfinder squadron goes to England next week.'

'That will be his squadron.'

'Is she serious about him?'

'I do believe she intends to go all the way with him tonight.' She was looking him straight in the eye when she said this. He couldn't match the words to her way of talking. Like the Mennonites you saw on a Sunday driving through East Atlanta, sitting straight-backed in an old-fashioned car looking forward, the women in bonnets, the men black-suited. Her voice like theirs. You couldn't imagine it other than level-toned, gravely cadenced.

Margaret and her pilot started to walk away from them down the street. Hooper knew the stories. He'd seen them on his journey here. Men standing alone on runway aprons. Women with suitcases at provincial train stations, bound for the terminals and ports, the rainswept places of embarkation, leaving under cover of the blackout. Going because they had to. Down the track all the dark stations where the shadows of desire are. Men and women with leavetaking in their eyes.

He had never heard a name like hers before. Elspeth. He told her that it belonged with the names of women in the Old Testament. Those who were barren, those who rent their garments, wives to men with burning eyes. She said he was more right than he thought but that his words were rich coming from a man who was named for an angel.

She was walking with him. She carried a small black patent handbag, churchy-looking, he thought. She held it with both hands in front of her. There was no one else on the road, mist in the iced ditches to either side of them, no masthead lights beyond the bar, the Haulbowline lamp quenched because of the war.

'What do you do?'

'I work a movie camera.'

'Like in the pictures?'

'A bit like that. It's for aircrews so they can learn how to drop bombs.'

'I can't think how that works.'

'The camera points down.'

'Show me.'

'I can't. You'd have to be on the base.'

'I can get on the base. You have to sneak in.'

'Under the wire. You'll get dirty.'

'I've been dirty before.'

The Bomb Loft

Hooper stretched out on the floor and put his eye to the bombsight. The footage was blurred. He told Elspeth to turn the knurled focus ring on the projector. She adjusted it and looked down on the estuaries giving way to dams, built-up areas, factory chimneys, the ghost landscape, death-haunted.

'Where are we flying tonight?'

'Look on the canister.'

'Essen. Duisburg. Dortmund.' The dead cities named. 'The Ruhr valley.'

'Why are we dropping bombs on valleys?'

'The factories are there. For planes and tanks.'

'Are there people there?'

'I reckon so.'

Hooper took the bomb release cable in his left hand. He bent his head to the iron azimuth. He pressed the button, thought he could feel the mid-altitude jolt of the bomb release.

'I feel sad for the people down there.'

'How's that?'

'This film's from 1943. That means they got bombed in that year, isn't that right?'

'Bombed in 1943 and forty-four and maybe in forty-two as well.'

Elspeth looked down, the landscape moving past under her feet as though it was something that had just been brought into being, the light moving across her face. She was standing beside the projector in the light behind the lens, the close-to-molten glare, so that he could see the bones in her face and the shadows made by them, some arch starlet posed and lit, the selling already agreed, the price yet to be met.

'You look like somebody in a film.'

'If you say so.'

'I do. Some rich girl about to be taught a lesson, one of those films.'

'Can't be right then. I'm not rich. You ever see a rich minister's daughter?'

'That what your father does?'

'Ministers to the Elected Brethren. Minister Davidson.'

'I'll change the film then. Preacher's daughter meets soldier, goes to the bad.'

'You're laughing at me.'

'No I'm not.'

'I never seen the flicks.'

'The flicks?'

'Movies, you say.'

'There's no movie house here?'

'There is but I'm not let.'

'How come?'

'It's not in the Book.'

'Is dancing in the Book?'

'No, but Father doesn't know.'

'How come he doesn't know?'

'I get out the window.'

'Hope your father doesn't see the film.'

'What film?'

'There was a man there with a movie camera.'

'McKee. He owns the picture house. He's always filming. In case a girl's skirt flies up. He might get a flash.'

'A flash of what?'

'You know what, Mister.'

'You dance good for a girl isn't let.'

'Margaret showed me how. She's got a phonograph. You get these dance steps with dress patterns. You roll this paper out on the floor and feet are drawn on the paper. You put your feet in the feet on the paper and cha cha cha.'

'Sounds a fool way to learn dancing.'

'No it's not. I'll show you.' She climbed down the ladder to the bomb floor. She took an eyebrow pencil from her hand-bag and licked the tip.

'Don't,' he said.

'It'll rub off.' She started to draw footprints, first the female and then the male. Patterns she knew by heart. Across the canvas where the film unreeled, dance steps across the bomb runs, the smoking ruins, the lonely precincts of the old cities.

'What dance is that?' Hooper said.

'The one you were dancing in the club.'

'So it is, damnit.'

'Blasphemer.'

'Hard not to when you do something like that.'

'Show me the dance.'

'We got no music.'

'We don't need music, I'm in the choir.'

Hooper stepped forward to take her hand.

*

He walked her from the Bomb Loft to the end of the Avenue.

'You could do with learning a few more dances,' he said.

'It's a pity I'm not let. I could be the biz at it. The cat's pyjamas.'

'Me and you could be Ginger Rogers and Fred Astaire.'

'I heard of them.'

'They dance and sing.'

'I'd love to see them.'

'Ginger Rogers is on at the movie house on Friday night. You could come.'

'The Vogue?'

'I never noticed what the movie house was called.'

'I'd never be let.'

'Who would know? You could say you was helping with the volunteering like tonight.'

'People would see me.'

'Not if you went in at the very back.'

'I know what goes on at the back of picture houses, Mister.'

'How do you know that?'

'Just because I live in a preacher's house doesn't mean I don't have ears. You should be in the bathroom at the dances. Well goodnight, ladies. Nothing left to the imagination.'

'Well then a movie isn't going to put you to no eternal damnation.'

'What's the film called?'

'Lady in the Dark.'

'Is it any good?'

'I don't know. I ain't seen it yet.'

'Maybe I will.'

'Where will you say you were?'

'Margaret's place. She said she'd leave a window open for me. I do the same for her. Girls are like that, Mr Gabriel Hooper. Little sneaks, little minxes.'

'You all right going up that Avenue?'

It was long past curfew. The soldiers back in barracks. The women gone home to their beds. The trees of the Avenue black against the fresh fallen snow. She stepped away from him into the entrance of the Avenue. A twig snapped in the frost. Snowfall from a branch.

'Look,' she said. The outline of a woman's body where she had been backed up against a tree trunk and her warmth had melted the rime on the bark to an hourglass imprint of desire.

'How many of the trees have that shape on them?' she said.

'All of them, I'd say.'

'What do you think they were doing?'

'You know well what they were doing. It weren't dancing, that's for sure.'

She placed one foot in front of the other. She held up her arms as though to partner the tree shadows, to take what lead they offered.

'Does the dance have a name?' she said.

'Not that I know of.'

'Give it a name. It'll be our dance then.'

'I'm not good at naming. It's a thing they do in church.'

'And I'm a church girl? Fair enough I'll give it a name. The Vogue?'

'Like the movie house?'

'Like the pictures.'

He heard her whisper the time he'd given her, two beats to the bar, counting it out in the Avenue, dancing the Vogue away from him, swing out from open and reverse, the named steps, the night held close until she was out of sight, the steps in the snow as though danced by something unseen.

Shepton Mallet
21st January 1945

Davis said they could escape from Shepton Mallet. He stole spoons from the canteen. They could construct rudimentary digging implements. They could cut through wire, tunnel their way to freedom. Davis drew on all the prison lore he knew. Files could be smuggled in, bars sawn through. If Davis overcame the Padre then Hooper could steal his clothing and walk out through the front gate. Hooper saw himself running through open country, bloodhounds baying in the distance. At night he would sit at the window shivering, timing the foot patrols and the frequency of the searchlight.

'Once that searchlight gets you in the beam,' he said, 'that's it. Goodnight, Irene. But it won't get us.' There would be ruses, split-second timing. Two men on the run, the odds against them.

There were meetings with Phair but there was nothing to say. Phair would write the date and Hooper's name on a legal pad. He would start to add detail to his handwriting, gothic flourishes on the capital letters, ornate cursive strokes. His name started to look Germanic, to acquire bleak authority. It looked as if it belonged on parchment, on decrees of annulling, of striking down. Hooper thought that it was wrong that his name should become a cruel edict.

In the exercise yard other prisoners looked at him thoughtfully. There was an edging away. They gathered in groups at the side of the yard, watching him walk through the slush. He tried not to look at them. They were gathering reminiscences about him, seeing him as a regretful figure walking away from them in the rain. Two days before the court martial he was moved into a cell on his own. Davis said it was because they had seen him at the window watching the patrols and knew he was planning an escape but not to worry as there were always setbacks. Plans had to be foiled, reverses overcome.

Davis said they had to see themselves as plucky, up against overwhelming odds.

Hooper could not remember what Elspeth looked like any more. In the court papers she was referred to as the victim or Miss Davidson. In the court papers a kindly light seemed to shine about her. She was a comfort to the afflicted, a bringer of succour. Her father's statement said that she had often taken Sunday school and had stepped into the place of her lamented mother who had gone before them in Christ.

There were parts of the Minister's statement that would not be read to the court. When she reached the age of majority the custom of the Brethren required that Elspeth's mother would begin the weaving of her shroud as a reminder to her of her mortality and to whom she owed her earthly existence. The shroud was kept in a winding box in the kitchen and Elspeth's mother was buried in it at the age of thirty-one. The Minister said that when Elspeth was fourteen she too had started to weave her shroud for one knoweth not the day nor the hour.

Reveille had sounded. Hooper was dressed. Stood to attention with the toes of his boots on the brick line midway across the cell, awaiting inspection. The door opened. An officer he had not seen before stood in the doorway. He looked Hooper up and down. If he had not been wearing a uniform Hooper would have thought he was Pierrepoint. He had the look of an itinerant hangman. A traveller through empty shires at night, a man who sat alone in provincial hotel rooms, his trade plied in the hours before dawn. A long pockmarked face unmoving, a backwoods gravity in his stare. Hooper stayed at attention.

'The Negro is given to concupiscence,' the man said.

'If you say it, Sir.' A warder carrying Hooper's breakfast tray was standing behind the man.

'I will pray for your soul, Hooper,' the officer said. He stood aside to allow the warder to enter. When Hooper looked up he was gone.

'Who was that?' he said.

'Captain Dupont,' the warder said. 'The prosecutor. He don't lose many.'

Hooper had not believed in the devil before, the figure his grandma had depicted as an urbane figure in a sharp suit and moustache, a riverboat gambler who would game for your soul, all to play for on the turn of a card at midnight, a smell of sulphur hanging in the air. He thought now that there might be other devils, imps of pinching and sneaking. They could have a long pockmarked face. They could be envoys of disappointment.

Thirteen

Morne
25th November 2000

Cole woke and put his hand on the iron radiator and took his hand away quickly as though the thing had been cast in a cold foundry. He could see his breath in the room. He got up and dressed. The window was glazed with ice. He rubbed it. The slate roof valleys outside the window were abstract geometries of white. Someone rapped on the door. He opened it. Lorna the receptionist. The girl was wearing a white blouse and black skirt but did not seem cold. Pale scion to the frost, he thought, offspring to it. Her eyelashes were the colour of her hair so that she looked as if she didn't have any. Her eyes red-rimmed though he did not think she had been crying.

'You're leaving today.'

'I want to extend the booking.'

'We need the room.'

'I can take another, anything you have.'

'We're fully booked.'

'There's nobody but me staying here.'

'We're fully booked.'

'Is there anywhere else in town?'

'We're the only place. Breakfast finishes in twenty minutes.'

Cole drove to the coroner's court and parked across the street. The roadway and pavements had been gritted. There were few cars on the road, two refrigeration units passed on the way from the harbour, salt spray thrown up from the rear axles. He saw Kay open the library, a swim bag over her shoulder.

At 9.30 the coroner's court doors were opened. The court was Victorian red-brick with leaded lights in sombre colours in the front door and porch windows. There were decorative roof peaks and turrets so that it looked as if the building belonged in a municipality where laws of necromancy were enforced.

A court usher in uniform told Cole that normal court sittings had been suspended due to the weather. His uniform was creased and the brass buttons tarnished. The usher had to check his counter list to confirm that the inquest into the death of a person unknown was still scheduled in court three. Upritchard and Lynch were in place in the public gallery when Cole entered the courtroom. There was a tall woman sitting in the public area beneath Cole. She was wearing a beret and a black fur coat. Corry on the bench. Lynch was called to the stand and read out an affidavit detailing the finding of the body.

'The purpose of this inquest is to ascertain four matters. Who the deceased was. Where they died. When they died and how they died. Sergeant Lynch, do we know the identity of the deceased?'

Lynch stood.

'We do not, Sir.'

'Do we know where the deceased died?'

'Enquiries are ongoing, Sir.'

'Are we aware of when the deceased died, or the cause of death?'

'We are awaiting the carrying out of an autopsy to find the answers to those questions. There are issues relating to the location of the body and the effect of substances in the ground.'

'Chemical waste.'

'The body has been exposed to certain processes. It may be difficult to ascertain a time of death and a cause.'

'There is a suggestion that the death may be historic?'

'The circumstances point towards that conclusion, Sir. The aerodrome was constructed hastily. Many young women remain unaccounted for at that time. There were liaisons with military personnel and it is assumed that many followed their beaus to England and thence to the United States.'

'Full investigations have not been carried out, nor has there been an autopsy. We cannot assume that the woman died where she was found. Therefore this inquest is adjourned until the fourth of next month.'

Corry stood up and left the bench. It was the court process Cole had expected. Dusty, hesitant, shorn of majesty. The shuffling of papers in empty provincial courtrooms, an atmosphere of ruin in progress, of lives on the slide. He thought of the girl in the hospital morgue. The embalmed reek of the remains, the half-preserved organs in their bone case. The hands clawed and reaching as though a part of death had been held back from her and she sought it. He knew she would come for him at night, the face in rictus, hanks of hair adherent to the skull, something akin to lasciviousness about her, grasping, unspeakable.

He wondered if he was the only person in the courtroom who felt it. The tall woman stood and turned to go. The high cheekbones defined with circles of rouge, her face powdered into the hairline, the eyes deep sunk.

'You know her?' the usher said.

'She's the Matron.'

'Matron of where?'

'Matron of the hospital when it was a home for troubled youth. Also wife to the esteemed Resident Magistrate, Isaac Corry.'

The woman stood with her shoulders back and started to walk towards the doorway. Tall, arch, beyond consolation. Cole knew she felt it too.

Lynch was standing in the foyer. His face raw. He rubbed his lips with a chapstick. Cole saw eczema on the back of his hands.

'You got what you come for, Cole,' Lynch said, 'time to get on your bike.'

'I don't like driving in bad weather.'

'You'd be nervous of it.'

'I would.'

'The town looks after its own, Cole.'

'I'll tell the girl in the morgue.'

'She'll have her day. After you're gone. You overstepped the mark. The girl is nothing to do with you. State your case on your land if that's what you're really at and get out.'

Outside he watched the Matron move down the empty street, her back slightly arched. She looked like the last descendant of minor nobility.

Cole met Kay in the Legion at the harbour. There were sailors talking quietly at Formica tables. Boat crews landed that morning, coming in wearing oilskins, frost in their beards. They talked of Arctic waters sweeping in across the feeding grounds, deep water currents moving. Seabirds dropping dead on the deck from the cold. Fuel lines froze, pumps jammed with ice. They were nervy, a behind-the-lines look in their eyes. They talked about finding jobs ashore.

'I got thrown out of the hotel.'

'How come?'

'They said they were booked out.'

'You can stay with me.'

'In the caravan?'

'Until this weather is over. Until Lynch stops telling me to increase my security, people stop spying on me. Until people stop breaking into the library. I'm not going to ask you your business, Mister, just that you can keep your hands to yourself.'

'I can do that.'

She saw herself as self-reliant and Lynch's warning had changed that. She had placed around herself devices of warding, seashells on her windowsill, mementos, worn childhood objects. Things that had an earned and durable place in her life. The hiking boots under the coats in the caravan, the worn dressing gown, the scuffed and marked indices of everyday virtue.

'What happened in the inquest?'

'They postponed the whole thing. They're waiting for an autopsy. As I said, could go on for years.'

'You know the Matron?'

'I know of her.'

'You know things you shouldn't know, Mister. She borrows books.'

'What kind of books?'

'Romances. Old time. Wings of Desire, that sort of thing. Forbidden loves. Cruel deceivers.'

People from a long time ago in crinolines. A longing for stately times.

'She lives with the Magistrate?'

'No. She has a house on the Avenue. She left him, they say. Big place, only her in it.'

*

Dr Eugene followed the river path under the trees. The water frozen at the edges. A bench had been placed at the river's edge. The slats had been broken off and used to light a fire. There were cans in the ashes, the grass and vetches trodden down, condom wrappers on the path, locale of illicit couplings. He passed the silent and unlit Kingdom Hall, the river running between the hall and the workhouse graveyard, the plain stone grave markers white with frost. The trees leaned in over the path, the wood growing thicker towards the Avenue. There were owls here. They hooted from within the wood.

In the field to the side of the Avenue a farmer had hung shot crows on a dead branch and left them there as a warning to vermin. Long-dead, the black feathered corpses hung weightless and asway on their makeshift gibbet.

Eugene approached the Matron's house through the

out-offices to the rear. Slate roofs collapsed inward, rotted hay barns, old tractor parts and tyres in empty yards. The house beyond unlit, a two-storey stone building with diamond-pane windows in double peaks to the front. When he tried the front door he found it open.

It was a long time since he had seen the interior of the house. Moonlight shone on polished wooden flooring. Timbered ceilings edged with chiselled flowerlets he did not know the names of. An ornate candelabra stood in the window recess. The back of a chair etched with strange devices was silhouetted against the moonlight coming through the deep-set windows. Eugene heard her footsteps in the corridor. He waited for her.

'Dr Eugene.'

She bent and switched on a tasselled lamp. She stood under a bookcase filled with leather-bound texts. Missals. Tracts. Accounts of missionary expeditions. The writings of Martin Luther and John Calvin and other dissenters and schismatics. Beside the bookcase were framed photographs of early con-gregations. The women in long dresses with lace inlays, hair drawn back from their faces. The men in black, preachers, lawgivers in monochrome.

'Give it to me,' she said. She took the photograph from his hand, the emulsion cold though he had kept it in his pocket, the younger boy sundered from the older, staring at the cam-era with sombre, violated eyes.

'It's the boy, Cole. Where is he now?'

'At the hotel but they won't let him stay.'

'You may be right. I barely remember Cole.'

'They called him Ghost. A nickname. Look after Ghost. She said that to me.'

'Some children are ghosts.'

'Some children have to be.' They fade into surfaces, they become their own background. They never look up. They never catch an eye. That was what the adults were waiting for.

'One way or another they will put the girl back in the ground unnamed,' Eugene said.

'They'll try.'

'They did it before.'

'Not this time.'

'The home was a cruel place.'

'It was cruel because we allowed it to be.'

'We did our best.'

'Our best wasn't very good.'

Eugene walked to the back door of the room and opened it. She could hear his soft footfall through the cold unused pantries at the back of the house. The phone rang. Corry.

'Where are the letters?'

'Where they will do most good.'

'Most harm, you mean.'

'That depends.'

'I sent you away. I educated you.'

'You and the Brethren gave me all the education I needed before I went anywhere.'

'I trained you. Midwifery. Nursing.'

'And when I was away the Brethren had a wake for me. As if I was dead. They said the prayers for the dead. And you attended. My husband.'

'Was I not right? Did I not get a dead woman? Yet you came back.'

'Where else would a dead woman gain employment? You

ruined me.'

'Your own appetites ruined you. Nothing else. You defied the law of God and the law of man.'

'You and the Brethren ruined me.'

'You lay with another, like a beast in heat.'

'I lay with no one. It was a lie then and it is a lie now.'

'I rescued you.'

'You bought me,' the Matron said.

'I thought the price cheap for no one else would want you,' Corry said. 'I was mistaken in the price, not in the wanting.'

Outside Eugene passed the drawing room. He could see the Matron framed in the window in speech with her husband, the grey beau and his gaunt, faithless coquette. He could see the gesturing of the loveless, mouthing the words spoken before in other empty rooms.

Kingdom Hall
14th December 1944

The hall different then, the approaches better kept. 'The Wages of Sin Is Death' painted on the high north gable. The floors are of plain unvarnished wood. The Brethren's arcana are inscribed on silk squares and hung on the wall to either side of the pastor's table. There is a Star of David in faded blue, the hull of a wooden boat, a cedar tree.

The congregation enter the valley through a wooden gate, men in dark suits and women in headscarves and long dresses almost unseen as they descend through the trees on the river bank.

It is a corrugated-tin gospel hall, painted green and dry-lined. In December frontal troughs in the north channel draw cold wind off the granite escarpments of the mountain behind and down through the valley, and the tree branches whip backwards and forwards as though some great shambling thing is forcing its way through the wood. The hall moves in the wind. The timber floor flexes beneath the feet of the chosen, small dust vortices are blown from the gaps in the boards. The window glass shivers. The elders' voices are raised against adversity and the eternal night to come. The women are whispering. Something rumoured to have happened the previous night. *The Minister's daughter.* They tell their girls to stay away from the American soldiers. To get off the road and hide in the ditches when their trucks came along.

Wesley Upritchard had been Named the previous Sabbath. Isaac Corry had been Named. John Lynch had been Named. Davidson judged them amenable.

When the service had finished the Minister asked the boys to wait behind.

'Boys, I wish to speak with you.'

'Yes, Minister Davidson.'

'I have a gift to deliver and I need your help in an errand.'

'What is the gift, Minister?'

'It is the gift of righteousness.'

'Is that all?'

'It is all I have to give. Will you help me?'

'I'll help you, Minister.'

'And me.'

'No one else shall hear of this. Giving is best done without bragging.'

'No one will hear, Minister.'

'You have a bright eye, Isaac Corry. The Lord is bountiful to those who labour in his service. Can you tell me who was the wife of Isaac in the good book?'

'Isaac was wed with Rebecca.'

'Yes. Isaac was wed with Rebecca.'

They drove out to the aerodrome in Davidson's car. The boys sat in the back seat. They stopped on Hangar Road to the rear of the aerodrome. It had snowed at nightfall. On the ground they could see the marks left by night fauna. It had been a cold winter and the starveling creatures fled from their coming. In the long frozen nights tree trunks exploded with frost, half-dead birds were taken in their nests by mink.

The boys followed Reverend Davidson. From a distance would be seen the figure of a man walking upright with a bundle under his arm like a pedlar and three boys behind him, black shapes against the snow. Little winter foxes yapped on the tree line. They followed the perimeter fencing to the seaward end of the camp. The sentries were in their guard-house at the gate and made patrol every hour. The snow had hardened to ice where it had blown on the windward face of the fenceposts and the wind raised a moan from the strung wire so that the boys looked up, fearful.

The Minister paid no heed. There was a group of huts inside the wire with concrete walkways between them. The wind blew flakes of ice from the rusted strands of the fence. It felt to the boys as if they had stumbled on an abandoned settlement.

'Is there nobody in them, Minister?' Wesley said.

'The landing lights have failed and the ground crews are setting out fire buckets to guide planes in. The hut is empty. Take the parcel, John Lynch, and place it in the locker beside the occupied bed.'

'I'm afraid the black man will come back and catch me.'

'I told you, he is at work. Go and attend to your chore.'

The ground the fenceposts were sunk in had subsided and there was space between the bottom strand and the earth. Lynch moved on his back under the wire. He thought about returning to tell the Minister about the vault of stars. But he was a minister and would know about the vault and maybe would know the stars by name.

The Minister had warned him about the taint of the Negro, his race abandoned by God, and he thought he could smell it but then he knew it for the smell of new-planed timber and the earth that the hut stood on.

There was only one made bed in the hut with a tin locker beside it. He thought he'd take a souvenir off the black man and reached inside. There was an oilskin shaving bag containing a bar of coal tar soap, a bristle shaving brush, hinge-back razor and leather strop. Something rang against the razor tang when he moved the bag and he put his hand in. He felt the outline of a coin in the side of the bag and took it out. It was a silver coin the like of which he had never seen before and he put it in his pocket. He opened the bag the Minister had given him and put his hand inside. He was holding a woman's stocking, underthings recently worn, the musked remnants. He put the clothing back into the bag and pushed the bag into the locker.

When he crossed the threshold of the hut he felt that he

had stepped out into a land he had never seen before. Beyond the dark timber of the huts and the snowy ground he saw the white mountains and the gulf of black water between them. Above that the named galaxies on their round, each star a bright wire cut into the black sky. He looked right to the Minister, who stood against the trees as if the night was all of his making.

The boy turned to close the door then stopped as he heard a man's voice carried across the runway. The man raised a shout again, his voice carrying off the mountains, something ceremonial in it, some part of the night called to order. The man called again.

The beacons came afire as the tar barrels were lit in sequence, a torch handed down the line from hand to hand, one brazier to the next, a road of fire laid across the shallow, iced margins of the black lough. In the distance the sound of heavy bombers beat against the silent flanks of the mountains. Men's shapes moved against the tar barrel fires. Oily smoke gathered across the mud flats and channel approaches. The boy looked west as though squadrons of the night had been called. To the boy it seemed that the Minister stood at the apex of the flaming lines. No good would come of this night. The boy smelt perfume on himself where he had laid his hand on the inner garments. The Minister beckoned to him. He rolled under the fence and the three boys followed the Minister back through the trees.

Fourteen

The Magistrate's House
25th November 2000

Corry had the strong room built to house deeds and other documents that he did not wish to lodge with the bank. The room had been added to the warehousing at the back of his house. The warehousing close to the river bank, prone to flooding at the nearest point. Disused for years. Iron pulley housings seized with rust hanging over the river, wooden window shutters rotted and fallen inward. There had been trade along the river bank and now it was a commerce of the shadows and he did not like to think of what might be sent from one failed holding to another. What wares were trafficked. What trades were plied.

Corry climbed the interior wooden steps to the strong room, took the iron warehouse key from its hook at the back door. He visited the strong room several times a week. It contained his familiars, the sinners and the sinned against. He crossed the yard at the back of the house. Snow falling on the cobbles. Eyes watching him. There had been cats in the warehouse and his wife had fed them through the years, bringing fish discards from the harbour, and he had spoken to her about turning what had once thrived into a cattery.

The timber floorboards had been eaten away over the years and were riddled with woodworm. The dark smelt of corn and India meal. The storerooms watchful. Corry knew the joists to be sound and he put his weight on them.

The strong room steel-doored, the walls of reinforced concrete and asbestos. The deeds of multiple properties were held in locked cabinets. There was an iron safe set into the back wall. The home's personal files were held in ring binders. Corry carried them to the strong room table and started to read. Each file with a small photograph attached. Sombre children in monochrome. The foundling stare. Running through the dates, the ledgered lives, a miser's hoard of intimacy.

Each page was signed or initialled. Doctors, social workers, policemen. Corry had other files in the safe. He'd seen many of these people in his courtroom. Had fined them, sent them to gaol. They'd stood in front of him, grateful to him. He was there to listen to the tales of the lost. The domestic incidents, assaults, petty crimes. The wayposts of ruin. They wanted to be listened to. Witnesses for the prosecution in their own lives.

The safe lay in his eyeline. There was money in there. Land transactions recorded. Documents of confession and guilt brought to him by Lynch. The files of the Reverend Davidson and others. He got up from the table and entered the combination. He opened the door and removed the lower drawer and carried it back to the table. He took out a drawstring bag in black velvet. He shook the bag into the drawer and a silver coin fell out onto the brown cardboard file at the bottom of the drawer. Reay's medical file.

He lifted the silver half-dollar and felt the weight of it in his hand, the sense of debts falling due. He would pay for his sins and this was the currency they would be paid in. The Walking Liberty. Stolen by the Negro soldier, no doubt. He left the coin down and went to the river side of the warehouse to look out over his town, but it was hidden from him, curtains of snow drifting through the empty window openings. There were slates missing, areas of powdered snow on the boards. There were footprints on the snow other than his. He looked up from the footprints.

'I know you now,' he said. 'It took me a long time, but I know you now.'

Fifteen

At the sound of the back door, Lily put her work away. Downstairs she come two at a time to see Kay stood there. Smell the night off her. Smell the cold.

'No heat gone to loss tonight, Lily.'

'Froze land. Froze beasts.'

'Froze indeed, Lil. What are you at?'

'At nothing.'

'You always hide something when I come in.'

'Not me hide nothing.'

'You're a sly dog sometimes, Lily.'

'It my sleep clothes.'

'The shroud. Is that it? I heard the yarns about the Brethren. Lily, you don't have to make a shroud for yourself. It's an old superstition.'

'You smell fear.'

'Don't change the subject.'

'Tell me.' Lily touched Kay's wet hair.

'I didn't know it showed. There was someone at the pool tonight watching me.'

There had been small waves on the black surface of the pool, chevrons of light defined by the masthead arrays of the docked trawlers a hundred yards distant. Ocean debris on the seaward walkway. Seaweed, shingle churned from the ocean bed, trawl fragments, sections of ship cable, broken fish boxes. She stood at the Victorian kiosk, the cupola broken and askew. The metal of the high board had begun to fail, the structure tilted to one side. Kay undressed in the roofless ladies' changing rooms. She could see the detail in the decorative mouldings, pagodas, women with eyes downcast, the chinoiserie in decay.

Kay lowered herself into the water close to the sluice. You could feel the tidal race on the channel side, the deep-water shingle grind against the concrete base of the pool wall.

A few others swam in the pool during the autumn and winter. Men and women. They did not speak among themselves. They had time for their own hardship alone. They came up out of the changing rooms as though last chances were involved. To pit themselves against the substance of the world. They looked ready to invoke old weathers, storms, epic events, fronts moving down from the north, isobars packed tight, old voices howling in the storm-lit interior.

She swam twenty lengths of the pool, turning at the diving board, bracing for the kick-off against the spent tiling, feeling slime on the soles of her feet. On the twentieth length she stopped. She was in the deep end, her legs hanging straight down, her head and shoulders above the water. She thought that there was someone there outside the lights. She had seen something as she swam, her eyes opening on the up-roll. Not a movement but an elaboration of the dark.

*

'Don't go to pool night-time,' Lily said.

'I have to go to the pool at night. It's the best time. It's lit. There's people at the harbour.'

'Was this man?'

'I never saw who it was. Just someone outside the light.'

'Run you?'

'That's what I did.' Putting her tracksuit over her wet costume in the roofless changing room. The vault of the sky above her. You had to cross the pool to reach the exit. The bent cupolas and Chinese lanterns against the harbour light like the skyline of a night city. There were broken deckchairs, the rusted metal frames of loungers, rusted welding equipment on the forecourse. You had to walk under the shadow of ruptured sun awnings. The dark behind empty windows and doorframes.

'I can't stop swimming, Lily.'

'Not safe. Where your man?'

'I don't have a man.'

'Got you man eyes. Man keep you safe.'

'What about you, Lily?'

'What man marry me?'

'You had your day.'

'No day. No man.'

'Suit yourself.'

'Yes. Suit me.'

'I'm away home.'

'Home you.'

'Lock the door after me. Keep the range lit. I'll call in tomorrow when you're in better form.'

'Rid me of you tonight Tango Zulu.'

'Rid me of you too, Lily. Never seen you cross like this.'

'See nothing Kay. Hear nothing Kay. Know nothing.'

Lily bolted the door when Kay left. She went to the Hope chest again and started to work. Sew and pick. Pick and sew. Each stitch by hand. The sleevework finish now. The bodice to work on. Take so much time. Be care not to prick finger. The white's the white of gull in the channel. It's the white of frost. There's hem to be done and panel on the front, and neckline and skirt to the heels. The hawk's froze stiff on the outhouse door. Yellow hawk be the dark. Bad to chase Kay. But Lily has no choice. Lily has errands to do in the night.

*

Kay thought at first that it was one of the caravan noises, the wind rocking it on its chassis, the aluminium sidings contracting in the cold, dry grass stems rustling in the crossbeams, the cold night's plainsong. She got up and went to the door. There would be a neighbour from one of the other caravans with an emergency, a husband taken ill, a pipe frozen. One of the few who stayed through the winter. Distant figures on the dunes. Hardy retirees pitting themselves against the forlorn. She put her hand on the door latch then waited. She called through the door and heard Cole. She opened the door.

'You look froze. I didn't think you were coming.'

'My car wouldn't start.'

'You walked?'

'Yes.' The road slick with ice. The aerodrome hangars vast and silent. The huts of Niggertown like abandoned shanties. Jack chain still hanging over the pit from where the girl's body had been taken.

They sat at the banquette table. She was wearing a dressing gown. She put her arms around her knees, put her chin on her knees and watching him drink tea. The gas fire hissed. She wore no make-up. Her hair was tied back with a hairband. He thought about teenage moments. Finding yourself alone, the moment worked towards, schemed at, the idiom of glancing touches.

'What's going on?'

'What do you mean?'

'The break-in. The way Lynch was. I wish they'd never found that girl. I wish they'd take her away. Something is loose in this town. I keep hearing things at night.'

'Snowstorms loose in the town by the sound of it.' He pulled back the curtain. Snow being blown across the beach and through the rows of caravans in the dark as though through an abandoned settlement. Snow gusting under the streetlights and against the corrugated sides of the Lighthouse cafe. The beam of the Haulbowline light just visible as it turned, its foghorn muffled and growing fainter, a lone baying as though being carried away from them out to sea.

'I want you to read the document that was left at the library, the Statement of Facts.'

She handed it to him. He sat on the edge of the banquette

to read it. When he had finished he held it up to the light. It had been signed at the bottom, the name illegible. The letters in blue ballpoint, frail, the pen not borne down on, the letters almost not formed. The words a blue graze on the paper.

'The preacher's daughter.'

'What?'

'Davidson. He was the old minister of the Elected Brethren.'

'Before Upritchard?'

'Different times, different man. Davidson was hellfire and brimstone. There's talk that there were shunnings.'

'Shunning?'

'You're banned from the church. Cut off from God. Cut off from the light.'

'Looks like this Hooper was going to get cut off from the light as well.'

'I wonder what happened to them.'

'Somebody wants you to know. Went to the trouble of breaking in and leaving the Statement of Facts.'

'I don't feel all that comfortable with it.'

'Neither would I.'

'I don't know what it means.'

'Or you don't care.'

'Maybe.'

'Something to do with your exhibition?'

'I don't know.'

He slept on the couchette in old cotton sheets, much-washed. A smell of coal tar soap he remembered. It evoked breathless trysts, a girl held against sun-warmed planks. The sweet discarded moments.

He woke to the radio. The weather closing in. Road and school closures, the sound of last-transmission static. You found yourself thinking of planes going down, ships in trouble far out at sea. Kay had put a kettle on the gas stove. She was wearing the dressing gown, old cotton socks gone threadbare at the heel. She bent to light the gas, brushing hair out of her face, holding her lower lip between her teeth. How she saw herself, given to small intent gestures, the blemished self put to work.

'The town will know you're here.'

'How come?'

'Upritchard has a camera in the Lighthouse cafe.'

'He has a camera?'

'It's supposed to be security for the caravan site.'

'Is it?'

'Not unless they need security against me. It's pointing at the front of the caravan.'

'What sort of town is this?'

'It's a place, like every other place.'

'I don't think so.'

She sat on the edge of the banquette, pulling on jeans under the dressing gown, lying back to button them so that she was stretched out across the bottom of his bedding. Beneath the dressing gown she was wearing a faded t-shirt, bra strap showing through the material. He wanted to reach out and touch her back. He wanted these makeshift intimacies extended to him.

'You see outside?'

He sat up and moved back the curtain. Snow drifted against the caravans, the ground frozen hard to the sea's edge. The sea grey, still, close to freezing. She knelt on the bed beside him.

'Looks like the Arctic.' The caravan park redolent of lost expeditions, crews stranded in distant bays, supplies dwindling, the pack ice closing.

'Four or five inches is what they say. Drifts.'

'I see the way people look at you. They think you're hiding things. They think you're not what you look like.'

'Who is?'

'I read the things you were looking up. Nothing to do with who owned the aerodrome.'

'And?'

'Who are you looking for?'

'You want me to tell you?'

'No. Not now. I can carry my own baggage. I don't want to carry yours.'

'Fair enough.'

'I'm going to work. You want to stay here?'

'I'll come with you. I can try to start the car. Get my bag from the hotel.'

The sandy ground outside the caravan gone iron in the cold, granulated, turned to grit. The windows of the Lighthouse cafe frosted. Her post box a biscuit tin on a stick. She reached inside and took out a white envelope, unaddressed. She opened the car and started the engine and they waited for the windows to defrost. She opened the envelope. It contained a single sheet of jotter paper, flattened along sharp creases as though it had been pressed in a book over time. She opened it out.

Get out you hore written across the lined paper.

'When was the last time you looked in the post box?'

'Yesterday. When I got back from work.'

'Somebody was here in the middle of the night.'

'In the storm.'

'Yes.'

'I don't know what any of it means.'

He knew what it meant. He'd seen this kind of thing before. The anonymous letter. Words scrawled on walls and doors. Blackballed, shunned. Go back to where you came from. He knew how it worked.

Get out you hore.

She put the letter in the envelope and put it in the glove compartment.

'You could give it to Lynch.'

'How do I know Lynch didn't put it there?' She started the car. The snow on the road not yet packed down, easy to drive on. Snow drifted against the aerodrome buildings with nothing to stop the blizzard funnelling down the lough and blowing across the empty acres. She turned on the radio. Snow ploughs making their way across the high passes. Freeing stranded motorists.

'Stupid people,' she said. 'Getting stuck.' There would be a torch in the boot of her car, emergency tools. She would make provision against the world, make store against loss.

He took the letter from the glove compartment and unfolded it again.

'Can I?'

'You not read it right the first time?'

Something in the scrawled letters. Something in the ink, the ornate transgressive hand.

'It's the lawyer in me. Looking for guilt.'

'Not much guilt in that.'

'There's always something.'

'*Hore.*' Kay trying out the word. 'There's someone out there thinking that about you. What do they see when they look at you? Some porn thing? Should I have something hanging out? Should I be on my knees? Where's my lip gloss? My come hither look?'

'Upritchard told me that things move about under the ground at the aerodrome.'

'So they say. They put in fenceposts, string wire between them. Next morning you come back and the wire has gone slack. There was an old graveyard out there. It's on the maps. Who knows where those coffins are now.'

The restless sands, the underground shiftings.

'There's a lot of old machinery from the war buried. Planes too. Just dozed them into the ground where they crashed.'

The transmigration of the dead. Cole's gaze travelling across the snowed-on concrete. What was dreamed of in the ground? The flightpaths of the dead through the gravel.

The town streets were empty. The snow worked into ice on the pavements. He followed her into the library.

'Not much point in being open today,' he said.

'I want to open,' she said, 'that's the point. Will you leave if you get what you want?'

'What makes you think I want something?'

He went into the back of the library with her. A high-ceilinged room. A mid-Victorian gravity about it, the walls lined with plain bookshelves, meshed in.

'I've been here for a year,' she said, 'and I know what sort of town this is. If I was you I'd turn your back on it. Go back to Scotland.'

'Too late for that.' Lynch's voice. The policeman standing in the doorway.

'You want to borrow a book, Sergeant Lynch?'

'What makes you think that?'

'This is a library.'

'Not today. I want to borrow your friend. You could do worse than come with him yourself.'

'What's this to do with?' Cole said.

'It's to do with the body in the river. Do you have a book here about that, Miss Chambers?'

Sixteen

Shepton Mallet
24th January 1945

'I approached Captain Dupont to raise the issue of a deal on a guilty plea,' Phair said.

'Why would I deal when I never done anything?'

'It doesn't matter anyway. Dupont refused to make a deal. He is confident of a conviction.'

'So what do we do?'

'Go in there and tell the truth. Hope for leniency. There is nothing else we can do. Read this. The part at the end has obviously been added later, but there's nothing we can do about that.'

Affidavit given on 15th December 1944 by Margaret Reilly and read into the record of the Court Martial of Private Gabriel Hooper on 22nd January 1945

I Margaret Reilly do attest that the information rendered below is a true and accurate account.

Me and Elspeth were in the way of going to the social in Warrenpoint. Get the glad rags on. Supposed to be over-eighteens but we could always get ourselves looking older than we were, especially Elspeth. She could put on the airs of an older girl when she wanted to. Elspeth was good and fond of the dancing and the social was where the good bands were. The Melody Aces. The Blue Orchids. Them ones. It was a Yank dance and none of the locals went there. Suits me says Elspeth. She meant by that that her da was death on dancing and drinking and Satan's doings and would of killed her if he found out. What he doesn't know won't hurt him Elspeth says.

Me and her would dance together for a while. Give them a good eyeful of the goods was the way of it. You'd get Yank cigs and maybe a pair of stockings off them and many's the girl got more than cigs and stockings off them. We arrived at the premises at approximately nine thirty. The dance floor was full but we found a spot. It was hot though the night was cold outside.

I seen the Negro GI but Elspeth seen him first. He was sat on his own behind the others. He had this quiet way of looking sent the shivers down your spine. The brown eyes he had. Elspeth leans over to me and says you know what they say about a Negro and I says Elspeth you witch. He says he'd teach her this dance that they done where he come from. What's this dance called she said saucy as you like, and he says it don't have a name, mam. I can't believe he called me mam, dead respectful Elspeth said when she came back. The next dance was a ladies' choice and Elspeth said she was going to ask him and I says be careful. What do you mean? she says. First of all I says you must recall to yourself who you are and the name you could get. And I says can you not see the way the men are looking at him and looking at you. What care I for that she says with a laugh. What care I for that could have been Elspeth's words for life. But I cannot say I seen her dance with him.

It was put to me that I helped Miss Davidson and Private Hooper to obtain a seat in the cinema in the part that was known as Lovers Lane, which is the double seats at the very back. I wish to state very clearly that I was never in this so-called Lovers Lane, which is at any rate a vulgar term that only town girls would lower themselves to. Miss Davidson was aware of her place in society and would not be seen in such a place. I attended the screening of Lady in the Dark on 13th December 1944. At no point did I see Miss Davidson. At no point did I see the Negro soldier. I was shocked but not surprised when I heard what he done to Miss Davidson as he was a most lascivious dancer and possessed the vices of his race.

'The minister wrote that last bit,' Hooper said.

'How do you know?'

'It just doesn't sound like Margaret.'

'You can't stand up and admit to knowing her, never mind knowing her well. We have to leave it the way it is.'

'My neck's the only thing not to get left the way it is, by the sound of it.'

*

The light on in his cell all night. Hooper worked on his uniform. The blacking on the boots. The belt, the webbing, brushing out the tunic collars, the warder at the spyhole every hour. 'Don't know why they bother,' Davis said, 'whole point is keeping your neck in one piece. You're hardly going to do the hangman's job for him, are you?'

He was given breakfast in his cell. When he was called from the cell there were two marines in dress uniform to escort him. The warder inspected him, straightened his tie. Small gestures bestowed on him. The cell blocks quiet that morning. Faces at the window watching Hooper and his guards cross the courtyard, one of war's processionals, incidental affairs soon forgotten.

Hooper tried to walk the way Lindbergh would walk, rangy, big-boned, squinting into the sun. He'd walk into the court martial, look the prosecutor in the eye with a steady gaze, answer in an authoritative, panhandle drawl. *Not Guilty.*

The president of the court martial and two auxiliaries sitting at a plain desk, the Union flag behind them. Every time someone moved, a chair leg dragged on the wooden floor. A chill English light fell on the polished surface of the evidence table. Hooper stood to attention. The Adjutant General was a grey-haired man in his sixties, a gravel-voiced veteran, a colonel's stripes on his uniform.

If you looked out the window you could see the Mendip Hills and the Black Down. Beacon Hill darker than the rest, its tumuli and limestone abutments cruel pre-histories under the tree cover.

Under the authority vested in me. The proceedings getting under way. There would be the reading of the indictment. There would be half-understood processes. Hooper was asked his name and his rank. He had trouble speaking, standing upright. He felt like some eye-rolling Negro from the movies. He could hear Phair shuffling papers, talking to the Adjutant General. *If it please the court.* Hooper wondering where the fancy courtroom talk came from. *On the 13th December 1944 at the place known as the Avenue.* Dupont was on his feet now reading out the indictment. *The accused did knowingly.* Hooper was beginning to see the point of the language, the rhythms embedded in it. The deep, loveless chanting. *And with malice aforethought.* Around him in the court they were speaking the language of the dead. He felt the presence of his own death in the room, its cold, wintry smell. The others smelt it too. They had convened upon that very point. *Proceed by way of interrogatory. The victim a Miss Elspeth Davidson.* Hooper did not know if he moaned out loud or not. He heard the Adjutant General speak to Phair. *The accused will take the stand.*

'Repeat your name and rank.'

'Gabriel Hooper. Private.'

'You know why you are before this court martial.'

'I am but I never done—'

'Answer the questions, Private. Speak slowly and clearly.'

'Yes, Sir.'

'You were acquainted with Miss Davidson?'

'Yes, Sir.'

'Where did you meet?'

'We were walking home after the dance in Warrenpoint.'

'You missed the truck home.'

'Yes, Sir.' *Let the black bastard walk.*

'And by coincidence Miss Davidson had missed her bus.'

'Her friend never told her it was going.'

'Her friend Miss Reilly. Margaret Reilly.'

'Yes, Miss Reilly only had eyes for her airman.'

'So you walked home with Miss Davidson?'

'We just got talking is all.'

'Where did you go with her?'

143

'She wanted me to show her where I was working.'

'The Bomb Loft.'

'I done the projectors. She wanted to see.'

'How would you characterise your relationship with her at this point?'

'I never had no relationship, Sir.'

'I mean there was nothing between you?'

'We were friends, Sir.'

'You knew she was a product of a religious background.'

'She said to me her father was a preacher.'

'Would you say you respected her?'

'Yes, Sir.'

'Before you left her that night you made an arrangement?'

'That we would go to a movie. She'd never been to one before.'

'Who made the suggestion? You or her?'

'She did. Elspeth.' The name, the half-lisped syllables.

'You didn't go to the cinema though.'

'We did go.'

'According to the Reverend Davidson's deposition you didn't go to the cinema.'

'We went to see Lady in the Dark.'

'You think that the Reverend Davidson may be mistaken as to the night?'

'The deposition is accepted into evidence, Captain Phair,' the Adjutant General said. 'In addition I think we might accept the word of a man of God.'

'Yes, Sir.'

'Perhaps it would help if the Reverend Davidson's statement was read into evidence?' Dupont, the prosecutor.

'I think that is a good idea,' the Adjutant General said.

'I have it here,' Dupont said.

Affidavit of Elspeth Davidson through her father Reverend Davidson, made this day 30th December 1944 and duly sworn.

I do hereby swear and attest that the following is a true narration based on the account of my daughter Elspeth Davidson.

I am Minister of the Elected Brethren church in Morne. In such capacity I have tended to my flock for seventeen years. My daughter was born in the year of our Lord 1928. The Lord saw fit to take her mother from us two years later in 1930 and left me a poor sinner to the rearing of Elspeth.

From the first Elspeth was a godly child who attended to her schoolbooks and to Sunday school, for though she was under pain of chastisement I rarely had to lift rod or address a rebuke. She applied herself to the household duties of her mother as best she could. She was devoted to the spread of the gospel. The Brethren hall was her home and the mission field was her joy. Her desire oft expressed was to spend time as a missionary in the foreign field and she chided me for my weakness when I said I did not want to lose her.

Following the events of the night of 13th December 1944 I spoke with my daughter and ascertained the following facts.

She had met the Negro soldier and had spoken to him out of pity for his isolation in a strange land. She had served tea at a social occasion in Warrenpoint as part of her church duties. She had not in fact attended the dance as some had suggested. The question of her having danced with the Negro or with any other soldier does not arise. It is a forsworn activity for our congregation.

She did not attend the cinema with him. Cinema is also a forsworn activity.

Elspeth did not speak of what occurred in the Avenue that night nor did I press her. When she returned home that night she was in great distress, her clothes were rent and items of her apparel were missing.

I asked of her what had taken place and for a while she would not tell me, such was her shame, but the strength of God filled her and she spoke out plainly in the end. She said the Negro Hooper accosted her and dragged her into the Avenue. Despite her pleadings he persisted in his foul stratagem. She struck out, she struggled, I believe she would have succumbed to her own hand such was her revulsion at the deeds of the accused man.

He was as a beast of the field. His voice was lewd, his manner barbaric as is the wont of his race.

Elspeth said, Father, ask them to spare him, he knew not what he did. I mention this as evidence of the nature of her character, not in any way to mitigate sentence. Vengeance is mine, sayeth the Lord, and we are His instruments.

'There is the affidavit. Do you maintain that the Reverend Davidson is lying, Private Hooper?' the Adjutant General said.

'I ain't lying, Sir.'

'When you're asked a straight question I'd advise you to answer it yes or no.'

'No, Sir, I don't think the Reverend was telling no lie.'

'Then you must be lying or mistaken. Carry on, Captain Phair.'

'You maintain that there was no encounter in the Avenue

on the night Lady in the Dark was shown in the cinema?'

'No, Sir. I left her at the cinema and went back to my quarters.'

'That is the full of your account of the night?'

'It is, Sir. All that I done.'

'That is all then.'

The Adjutant General invited Dupont to step forward. The prosecutor sat shuffling his papers. Preparing his cross-examination, the steel-trap architecture of it. Standing up slowly. Taking on the look of a doleful southern preacher. Evil was a sad fact. He took no pleasure in seeing God's punishment meted out.

'You say you were at the movies?'

'Yes, Sir.'

'What film did you see?'

'Lady in the Dark, Sir. With Ginger Rogers.'

'The cinema owner states that Lady in the Dark did not commence screening until the day after you were arrested.'

'That's not true, Sir. That was the film I seen and that was the night I seen it and I seen it with Elspeth.'

'Refer to the young lady as Miss Davidson, Private Hooper.'

'Miss Davidson, Sir. She was with me.'

'The policeman on duty will agree with the cinema owner.'

'That isn't true, Sir.'

'Her father's affidavit states that she did not attend the film.'

'That's not true either, Sir.'

'At the risk of repeating the words of the defence, you would accuse a minister of the church of telling lies?'

'He might just be mistaken, Sir.'

'You think he would be mistaken regarding a matter of this nature?'

'I guess not, Sir. I just know that me and Miss Davidson went to the pictures that night.'

'Did you think she was pretty?'

'Who, Sir?'

'Miss Davidson. Did you think she was pretty?'

'I don't know, Sir.'

'You're a normal young man. You know when a girl is pretty?'

'Yes, Sir, I guess.'

'Your statement says that you danced with this pretty young girl Miss Davidson at the soldiers' dance in Warrenpoint prior to this assignation you said you had at the cinema.'

'I didn't want to. She come over. It was a ladies' choice.'

'Why did she come over?'

'Maybe because I was a good dancer.'

'You were watching her before that.'

'I never seen her before she walked up to me.'

'So you say. But she was a pretty girl. Everyone notices a pretty girl.'

'Might be.'

'Did the dance have a name?'

'A name?'

'Did it have a name, Private? The Jive? The Jitterbug?'

'Where I come from it had no name. She gave it a name.'

'She?'

'Miss Davidson.'

'What did Miss Davidson call it?'

'She called it the Vogue.'

'After the movie house? She named it after a venue forbidden to her by her religion?'

'Yes, Sir.'

The prosecutor stood over the evidence table. He moved his hand over the clothes there as though he offered them for sale. The court was meant to see the Negro looking. A woman's underthings. Some kind of satin in them. Stockings and the belt that went around the waist. The little brass buckles making a noise when they were touched. He lifted one of the stockings and held it up. Flimsy and scented. The GIs got them for the girls on the black market and there was something illicit about them, traded in the dark. The prosecutor let the stocking slip from his hand, the silk trailing through his fingers in an intended burlesque, coiling on the edge of the desk, gripping the wood then slipping off onto the floor. The prosecutor looked down. The polished tips of his shoes touched the stocking, the erotic discard, an abandon brought into the court. It lay on the parquet for the rest of the cross-examination, the interior garment, carrying with it the underskirt heat.

'Do you recognise these things, Private?'

'No, Sir, I don't recognise them.'

'You should do. Miss Davidson was wearing them the night you waited for her on the Avenue.'

'I don't know, Sir.'

'How did you get back to base on the night of the alleged movie date?'

'I walked, Sir.'

'There is no record of your return to barracks.'

'I missed curfew, Sir. I come in under the wire.'

'You missed curfew or you had something to hide. Sneaking under the wire like a thief in the night.'

'No, Sir. I got in under the fence because I missed curfew.'

'You had Miss Davidson's underthings in your pocket. The foul deed had already been committed. You thought you'd keep a souvenir of her. In your arrogance you thought you had got away with it.'

'I told you. I never seen them underthings before.'

The prosecutor turned to the court. The word in the Negro's mouth. *Underthings.* The thought of the girl exposed. Violated. Flimsy things torn and pocketed. The cross-examination leading towards this moment.

The prosecutor sat down beside Phair. He leaned over to him and whispered.

'Your client just hanged himself out of his own mouth.'

Seventeen

Morne
26th November 2000

Scene of Crime Photographs:

Image #1

The town river as seen from the Hollow. There is snow on the river margins and ice on the standing pools. The river in mid-winter spate. Held back by the buttress of the bridge. Bone-coloured rocks just under the surface. Nothing can be seen of the sky, the camera pointed downwards at the foot of the warehousing, the broken jetties and long-gone walkways, the loading piers swept with water. These are the tidal reaches, the surge from the river mouth, the estuarine deeps, sea-things carried up with the surge out of their own depth and meaning. Drowned seagulls, broken fish boxes, the tide-borne detritus of the shoreline.

Image #2

The photograph is taken from the Stonebridge. The warehouses are on the northern bank of the river. The Hollow is opposite, overshadowed by the hotel. There are a few cars in the Hollow, batteries gone dead in the cold or unable to climb the small frost-covered hill onto the street. The sky beyond reflects the colour of the sea and there are dark trails of marine diesel exhaust where trawler engines run. One of the swimming pool cupolas in the foreground. The blue slate roofs of the Mall, lost townships in the still icy mist.

Image #3

A tree has been swept down the river and lodged against a jetty's iron frame. Black boughs aloft. A body caught in the branches. The wrought shapes of the branches hold the torso. The current rolls the body from side to side. Dark clothing. Hard to tell if it is man or woman. A town derelict old before his time, weathered, lost in vagabondage.

Image #4

Taken from the jetty. A man in a black suit face down in the water. A branch has caught his left sleeve and holds it up in the air as if in defiance, as if there was anything there to be defied. The roll of the current lifts the grey head every few seconds and then plunges it back down into the current. His shoes and socks have been carried away by the current and his feet are asway like white winter flowers amid the black tree boughs. On the margin of the photograph are a coil of nylon climbing rope and the grab bar of an aluminium ladder. A recovery attempt being made. Volunteer crews trying to reach the body before it breaks away from the tree and is carried downstream and out to sea.

Image #5

The body has been brought ashore. The dead man is lying on his back on the jetty. The black suit. The chill, dead flesh. Isaac Corry looks like a victim of a political assassination, a man gunned down in the plaza, hapless, black-suited. The photograph taking on the quality of evidence.

Forensic Mortuary Security Cam:

The undertaker Morgan backs the Mercedes hearse to the rear entrance. The black tin coffin is slid onto the morgue gurney. The footage is flickering. The speeds are always wrong. Everything's silent-movie era. The undertaker's a gothic villain in a top hat. Death's attendants coming for Corry at ten frames a second.

Morne Police Station, Interview Room
1.40 p.m.

Present are Kay Chambers and Detective Sergeant John Lynch. Ms Chambers has declined legal representation.

Where was John Cole last night?
    He was with me.
    Was he now?
    He was.
    What time did he get there?
    I don't know. Maybe one o'clock.

Did you have relations?

What sort of a question is that?

It's the question I'm asking.

None of your business what we did.

Did you notice anything unusual about him when he came in?

Like what?

Was he agitated? Were his clothes clean or dirty? Had he any scratches on his face, anything that might indicate a struggle?

He was cold.

Did he have anything with him?

What do you mean?

Was he carrying any documents? Was he carrying any form of bag which might contain documents?

He had nothing. Just a coat.

Could the coat have concealed documents?

I don't know. Can I go now?

You're not under arrest.

I know that. Which means I can go now.

If you want to.

Morne Police Station, Interview Room
2.35 p.m.

Present are John Cole and Detective Sergeant John Lynch. Mr Cole has declined legal representation.

Where were you last night?

I stayed with the librarian.

Kay Chambers?

Yes.

At her caravan in Ocean Sands?

Yes.

What time did you get there?'

Half twelve, one, something like that. My car wouldn't start.

Can you prove it?

Prove what?

The time you arrived.

I don't have to.

Can Chambers confirm it?

I'm sure she can.

There's something about you that reminds me of boys from the town coming through this room. Petty thieves, men who beat up their wives, drunk drivers. The kind of crime you get around here. And you're like them. Something in the eyes. Something that tells you not to believe a word that comes out of their mouths. If you told me it was night outside I'd go to the window and check before I'd believe you.

Is that tape still running?

Yes it is running, Cole, if that is your real name.

It is.

I was through your car. No driving licence. No bills. Registered to a hire company in Scotland.

You had no authority.

I am the authority. Strathclyde police tell me you're some class of a lawyer all right. Hanging around courtrooms offering your services to the lowlifes of the day. The lower the life the better he likes it is what they tell me. Not a proper solicitor they say. At home in the gutter they say.

I'm here to co-operate with you in a criminal investigation.

Co-operate my eye.

Charge me with something or I walk out the door.

Walk then. I have no charges for you and you know that. What I got is a drowned man.

If he's drowned, why are you questioning me?

Get out of here, Cole. You're nobody.

I'm an officer of the court.

Not here you're not. You see some kind of benevolent society for the likes of you here?

Morne Police Station, Interview Room
4.20 p.m.

Present are Lorna Annett and Detective Sergeant John Lynch. Ms Annett has declined legal representation.

My name is Lorna Annett. I am manager of the Roxboro Hotel in the Hollow, a position I have held for three years. On the evening in question I had been working in the kitchen and checking hot water pipes in case they would freeze in the wintry blast. The hotel was vacant at the time. I am reminded I had said that it was fully booked but that was a ruse to achieve the departure of an unwelcome guest. It is my habit to sleep in the hotel at night when on duty as there is no night porter. Several times I formed the impression that someone was at large in the corridors and passageways at night and though I called out there came no answer and fear was on me so that I locked and barred my door and sometimes remained without sleeping until first light.

I had left slops from the bar on the kitchen fire escape to empty them into the river below when the opportunity presented itself. When it was dark I stepped out onto the fire escape. The slop pail had frozen. The steps were slippery with ice and caution was my guide. The fire escape was in a line with the windows of Mr Corry's warehouse across the river. Sometimes at night there would be a bare light in the warehouse window though it was many a long year since a boat come up the river to be loaded there. I emptied the pail against the round of ice that had froze at the top of it. I was on the turn back into the hotel when I looked across and seen someone standing in the pulley doors straight across from me, the best part of twenty yards across the torrent. I was near witless with fright and near let pail and all fly. It seemed neither man nor woman but something ungodly, a shadow raised up and set to unclean purpose. It remained still and neither did I move, being froze to the spot. I might have stood there for all eternity had not the pail fallen from my hand and gone to loss, clattering on the ironwork of the fire escape and then swept beyond redeeming in the river far below. When I lifted my eyes from the flood I seen that the shadow was gone though the light was still lit and I could see the room behind empty of all that lived.

*

Cole walked down the hill from the police station, snow impacted on the pavement. He felt like he'd been in the police station for a long time. He felt like a prisoner released after years, belongings in a cardboard box, clothes a little out of date. He understood how you might feel, suddenly unboundaried, the world too big for you. Wanting to reach out and feel the sides of things, to be hemmed.

The library steps had been salted. He could feel the granules under his feet. He could feel the courthouse that it had been, the consequence of it, miscreants led up the steps into the penal gloom.

Kay in his basement room, at his desk, going through the files he had left there.

'I've never been questioned in a police station before,' she said.

'I'm sorry.'

'All right. I need to know about you now. Doctors' records? Dental records? What are they for?'

'I'm trying to identify the girl found in the sandpit.'

'Why?'

A client asked me to look into a runaway from the hospital.'

'Why would anyone run away from hospital?'

'It was a children's home between 1970 and 1988. There were allegations of abuse. There were absconders.'

'You think the girl in the pit is your runaway?'

'I don't know. I can't get the material I need. The files have been gone through and any reference to her taken out. I'm not sure if the dental records are any good. There's no chain of custody. Anyone could have tampered with them.'

'Including you.'

'Yes.'

'What's her name?'

'Reay Wilkinson.'

'Who's looking for her?'

'I can't say.'

'Jesus Christ.'

'I'm not the only one in this town hiding something.'

'You can say that again. But you're the only one stayed in my caravan last night that's keeping secrets from me.'

'Client confidentiality isn't keeping secrets.'

'You don't talk about your past. Your family. Girlfriends. Where you went to school. Where you went to college. Look at me. I swim. I live in a caravan.'

She was looking up into his face. Her hair pulled back from her forehead. There were lines at the corners of her eyes, the plain clip holding her hair back, tokens of earnestness. Freckles, a small scar on her temple, something from a childhood fall. There would be illnesses, holidays in a familiar place, first boyfriends. The detailed happenings recorded and set aside against uncertainty. What you got in families, fondnesses passed from one to the other. This is me, aware of my limits. Life set out with what's attainable.

'I'm sorry,' she said, 'I don't have a right to shout at you. I'm scared. I don't know what's going on with all of this. I need to show you something.'

A silver coin in her hand. Her hand was small and the coin covered the palm, bright and untarnished. It looked like a coin from a tale, some hoarded weregild.

'Where'd you get it?'

'It was on my desk this morning.'

A goddess on one side with the sun at her feet. An eagle on the obverse.

'A silver half-dollar. I looked it up,' she said. 'It's called Walking Liberty.'

'What kind of date?'

'1943. The war years. The goddess is Liberty, I think. Something to do with the war.'

'Telling you something.'

'Telling me nothing.'

'You don't know that.'

'Show me,' she said.

'What?'

'This home you're talking about. Show me.'

'The library is still open.'

'I'll close it.'

They walked on fresh snow to the bridge on the meeting house road. She put her arm through his.

'Don't get ideas,' she said.

At his car he knelt to look at the door lock, the paint around it gouged, the chrome keyhole dinged and sullied where it had been forced. Lynch. Inside, the glove box had been emptied onto the floor, the back seats lifted from their flanges and not returned. His bag was in the boot, clothing thrown aside, rummaged through. He put the bag together. She was looking across the river at the hospital, stick nests in the pines, crows adrift like black charred fragments against the snow so she wondered what had burned to make such ashes.

He looked at himself in the wing mirror. He was unshaven, his shirt collar dirty, his eyes deep-sunk. The meeting house path took them along the river towards the hospital.

'Are we allowed up here?' she said.

'I didn't ask.'

'The dead girl.'

'She's in the morgue. In the basement. She's not dangerous.'

'Are you?'

'You wouldn't be with me if you thought I was dangerous.'

They left the path and walked through the limestone grave markers of the burying banks, soon lost under the Scots pines like shadowed remnants of the old forest, surrounding them with forebodings, old hauntings. At the top of the escarpment they looked down on the front of the hospital where a squad car had pulled up.

The undertaker Morgan held the door and the Matron got out. She stood by the car until Lynch joined her, then she moved with gaunt authority towards the hospital entrance.

'What are they doing?'

'Identification of the deceased, I'd say.'

'Do they still do that?' The theatre of it. Numbed amid the stainless steel and white tiles, clanking processionals, gurneys adrift on rubberised matting. Pallid corpse-faces turned up to the chill frosted air. Is this your husband, son, mother?

Cole brought Kay up the fire escape, the town below them snowbound like some far-off settlement, almost unseen in the scantling daylight. The fire escape swayed under their weight, the rusted members creaking like some tower of unreason, but she did not look down. He helped her onto the footplate at the top of the fire escape and pushed the door open.

They stood in the silent corridor.

'Should we be here?'

'The dormitories are this way.'

She followed him down the corridor. The doors on either side closed. The walls smelling of damp, paint peeling from the walls. Lines worn in the linoleum floor covering, thousands of footfalls passed along here over the years. There were far-off scuttlings in the roof space. He saw her glance into the dentist's surgery, the articulated arm of the dentist's light crooked towards them, the foxed leather of the dentist's chair. She shuddered. Some childhood fear brought alive, he thought, the child pinned down, worked on.

There were iron-frame beds in lines on either side of the dormitory. The painted frames were chipped and the metal springwork was rusted and bent. The narrow foam mattresses belonging to the beds were stacked to one side. The sprung bases of the beds had sagged so that they held the bowed shape of a sleeping child. There was a row of porcelain sinks under the windows at the gable end of the building. The chromium on the taps had oxidised down to the bare metal. There was brown staining on the porcelain of the sinks and staining from the copper piping on the wall tiles.

'Looks like the kind of place you'd cry yourself asleep,' Kay said.

Rain blew against the steel-framed windows above the sinks. Cole could feel the draught on his face from the gaps in the warped frames. It was always cold when the wind blew from the east.

There was a pressed-steel locker beside each bed. Cole counted the beds on the left side of the room then walked to the eighth bed down. He turned the side of the locker towards him. *Reay Wilkinson* scraped on the side of it with a compass tip. The name she gave herself ciphered with time and unknowable.

'This and the dental records are all I can find to prove she ever existed.'

Teenagers writing their names in toilet stalls. Carving their names on trees. You left clues behind you. Documented in outhouse doorjambs and toilet stalls. They scribed what there was of yourself. In case you got lost. In case someone might want to find you.

'Are there no more documents from the home?'

'You're looking at the documents.'

'It's very lonely.' She walked down the row of beds. The sides of each locker were written on. Girls' initials. Band names. Hearts. Boys' names drawn in bubble writing. Adolescent longing. What the heart wants. Male genitalia drawn in felt tip, crude, fetishised. *Slippy when wet.* The tenderness of girls, alone, crying in the dark.

'I don't like this place,' she said. 'Where did they go to be punished? They were punished, weren't they?'

'Couldn't have run the place without it. There was a punishment room. In the cellar.'

There were lockdowns for runaways. Removal of privileges for cigarette smoking. Older men waiting in the predatory shadows. Runaways returned by the police. Tales of innocence defiled.

'I think I'd like to go now.'

'Go where?'

'Anywhere but here.'

*

Corry's body had been laid out on a steel table in the morgue basement. Upritchard stood by it. He had a prayer book in his hand.

'My old friend,' he said. 'Salvation awaits him as it does the righteous.' The Matron brushed past him. The kingdom was not for the likes of Corry, she knew. Her neither.

Corry's hair had been parted on the wrong side. Faithless to the last, yet she looked to his fingers and thought back to when he had first laid hands on her. How he knew her. The things he said to her, the whispered defilements. The things he called her. *Used goods.* Given to him by her father. No man other than he would have her. He always had good hands. Long, interfering fingers. His face looked thinner, caved.

'Can I go into the house?'

'The Magistrate's house? Not until we're finished.'

'There are letters there.'

'There were all manner of documents there.'

'There were?'

'Someone's been through the safe.'

'All gone.'

'Looks that way.'

'In whose interest?'

'What?'

'Who would care? The past is done with and we are done with it.'

'The Lord forgetteth not.'

'He will not forget you Wesley Upritchard, you pious bastard.'

There was a squad car at the front of the Magistrate's house. The door taped off. Upritchard thought there should be people on the other side of the tape, whispered speculation, passers-by glancing up at the building, the tall cross-paned windows, the weathered plaster, the house left strange by

164

Corry's dying. They imagine the silent drawing room, the kitchen table still set, the death-prowled corridors and stairway.

Upritchard parked beyond the yellow tape. He walked to the door. A uniformed constable stood just inside the door, his tunic collar pulled up. Upritchard nodded to him. His father in the Brethren and his father before that.

'Sergeant Lynch here?'

'Upstairs, Reverend. He says not to let anyone up.'

'You don't bar the clergy. It is the wish of the widow that a verse from the Bible be read at the scene of her bereavement.'

'I'd say it's fine, Reverend. Sergeant Lynch is out the back.'

The strong room was a scene of plunder. The safe open, papers scattered. Lynch was on his knees gathering what he could. Deeds, testimonials, statements unheard in open court. Documents of sundering and confession.

'Do you think that everything that ever happened in this town got wrote down and Corry took a copy of it?'

'Looks like it.'

'Any money taken?'

'There's cash still in the safe.'

'Not thieves then?'

'No sign of forced entry.'

'What about your cameras?'

'Nothing. The snow hid everything.'

'Perchance he jumped. Perchance he sinned?'

'No chance at all.' Suicide not in the viewfinder for the opportunistic.

'Slipped?'

'Who ransacked the safe then?'

'Will you conduct forensics?'

'It's going down as an accident. No outside agencies.'

'Will the world outside not judge that expedient?'

'The world can judge away. Half the bones in his body was broke from the fall. Unless the inquest finds something else we can safely say it was an accident.'

'Who'll do the inquest?'

'Who indeed?'

'It's the work of Satan.'

'Satan should be at home among them documents.'

'There is only one man who might profit from the documents.'

'My money's on thon fly boy Cole.'

'Lorna expelled him out of the hotel. I seen to it.'

'Don't talk like you order what happens in this town, Upritchard. It's a long time since the like of you had the ordering of anything.'

'The Brethren are still amenable. The Brethren are still in my hand and God's.'

'Let's maybe leave God out of it at this time. God's going to have to look the other way. Shouldn't be too hard. He's used to it.'

'Where is Cole?'

'His car's still parked out the meeting house road. He's in the caravan with the librarian.'

'A man of retribution.'

'Maybe we have retribution coming.'

'Man is sinful. Retribution is mine, sayeth the Lord.'

'If so I'm waiting to get mine from the Lord, not from

Cole. You know that everything we ever done was locked in that safe?'

'I know. And I know that the front door was barred. Who would he let in at night?'

'Me and you.'

'Apart from me and you.'

'The Matron maybe.'

'Aye, the Matron. Was the widow Corry roaming the town last night?'

'He shut her out years ago.'

'Then it was Cole.'

'Why would he come after Corry?'

'I don't know. And if he's after Corry, chances arc he's after us.'

Eighteen

Pirnmill Aerodrome
15th December 1944

When Hooper woke up there were four MPs standing around his bed, figures in the dark. He got up on one elbow. From the north runway he heard a P-38's engines go from idle to taxi. It seemed he had been dreaming of flight.

'Well look who's woke up,' the nearest MP said.

'Man's entitled to disregard the dawn,' another said.

'May be his senses are disordered by the snow.'

'May be it don't snow in whatever part he was dragged up.'

He knew there were forms to be observed, laconic talk they felt themselves entitled to, homespun and cruel. He knew he would have to get out of bed and dress in front of them. Keep his eyes downcast, see only their boots and the floorboards. They'd tell him to hurry up, that they hadn't got all day to watch a Negro getting dressed, did he know how to tie his shoelaces, did he know there was a war on? He pulled his trousers on and stood up. He reached under the bed to get his boots. One of the MPs kicked them out of reach. He had to go down on one knee to get them out from under the bed, the MPs telling him to hurry. The word *boy* hanging in the air. The word *nigger*. He saw boots moving towards his locker, heard the drawer slide, his things picked through, his razor, his toothbrush.

'What's this? Negro been bookreading? Horseman of the King. Story of John Wesley?'

'Think you might be needing some of that good-living reading material.'

'Think you might be right.'

Hooper heard the book being thrown back into the drawer, glad it hadn't been taken, the last letter from his grandmother in it. The MP hunkered down and Hooper heard the locker door open, the MP grunting as he reached inside. The others went quiet. Hooper wondered if a senior officer had entered the room. There was something to be deferred to, the way the men stiffened, something more present that anyone else in the barrack room. A scent reached him, still bent under the bed, perfumed, ephemeral, close to the skin. He thought of Elspeth leaned in to him, close to him, not touching. The longing in what was withheld. Desire best told in its absence. Hooper standing up. The redcap was holding a girl's under-clothing in his closed fist, stockings, an underskirt, the shoulder strap and metal clasp of a brassiere.

'What we got here, soldier?'

'Nigger got him a girl.'

'Nigger got him the preacher's daughter.'

Outside it was barely dawn. The P-38 was in the air, turning to port against the mountainside, its exhaust a red-hot bar inset to the fuselage.

He remembered men walking home at night from the iron-works at Puritan Mill. A bus dropped them at the side of the freeway and they walked home on the margins, lunch pails under their arms. They wore hobnail boots with steel toecaps and every so often one of the young men would throw his leg back then kick forward and drag the hobnailed sole along the packed-down flint of the hard shoulder until sparks flared in the darkness. He stood for a moment staring up at the mountain, the flare of the exhaust flames arced across the dark slope as though something vast walked the valleys shod in flame.

*

That night the three boys meet on the Avenue. Close to curfew and there are only a few GIs and their girls among the trees. Other nights the boys would spy on the couples, hoping for a glimpse of thigh, the palm-sized white flesh above the stocking top crossed by the suspender strap. Boy talk. The diddies on her. The slips and brassieres, the flimsy belts, all the imaginings made real in the night-time Avenue. What favours they thought granted in the shadow of the trees. To be whispered to. To be pleasured in the dark.

'The redcaps took the black man away this morning,' Wesley said.

'Nobody says it's anything to do with what we done,' Isaac said.

'A girl was outraged,' John said.

'Was she?'

'Maybe done in I hear tell.'

'He done it then. The black man. They'll string him up.' John's face in the darkness.

'Why'll they hang him for that?'

'They'll think he robbed them off her when he was at his business.'

'He'll be dead and it'll be our fault. We put them things into his locker.'

'He'll be dead for thinking he can go near one of ours. If he was in the place he come from there'd be no court, there'd just be a branch and a rope.'

'How d'you know that?'

'Minister told me. Says it's God's justice. We are only his instruments.'

'When did you start talking to the Minister, Isaac?'

'He stopped me on the road this morning. He pulls up beside me in the car and tells me to get in.'

'You telling the truth so help you God?'

'Don't bring God into it, Wesley Upritchard. You don't know what God thinks. Minister says to tell nobody what we done, we were only bringing salvation to a wretch.'

'How does being hanged for something you never done bring salvation?' John said.

'Minister Davidson gave me this.' Isaac held out a black-bound book, the cover worn to the cloth of the binding through long handling.

'He gave you a Bible?'

'He gave me his Bible. He says we are required and solemnly bound to give our undertaking that we will not speak of last night until the time of Resurrection when the dead rise from the dust and walk in God's glory.'

'You're making this up,' John said. In the dark of the Avenue a woman spoke something inarticulate to the night. Voice was given to the profane doings of man and woman.

'This is a wrong place and it is a lewd thing you ask, Isaac Corry,' Wesley said.

'Put your hand on the book, Wesley.' Isaac held out the Bible. John took Wesley's right hand and placed it on the cover. Isaac put his own right hand on top. Wesley could not keep his hand still. He could see the words on the cover picked out in worn gilt, catching the moonlight as though the text and the glory within burned through. He knew his whole life would be wrong after this night. To be gathered here like thieves for the purposes of pledging, of that which once given could never be taken back.

'Repeat after me with your own name. I Isaac Corry do solemnly swear.'

'I Wesley Upritchard do solemnly swear.'

'I John Lynch do solemnly swear.'

'That by pain of eternal damnation . . .'

Corry's eyes shone in the dark. Wesley was moaning to himself, speaking in a tongue of his own invention fragments of half-remembered scripture, childish prayers.

'Say the words, Wesley,' Isaac said. He could see the whites of Wesley's eyes. 'That by pain of eternal damnation.'

Wesley moaned and said the words. The soldiers and their girls had gone quiet and Wesley imagined that they had paused to bear witness to the three boys, knowing what it was like to be sworn in, bound over for their lives.

When they had done swearing they took their hands away from the book. John said they were a secret society. That they could prick their fingers with a knife and mingle their blood. He took a wood-handled penknife from his pocket and opened out the blade, the edge stropped.

'We did already swear on the good Book,' Wesley said,

'blood's not more binding.' His own language scriptural, elevated. His face looked thinner, honed, the face of a minor prophet, the eyes deep-sunk.

'He's right,' Isaac said, 'give us that knife here.' John turned the knife and gave it to him, handle first.

'We've need of something to remind us what we done here the night.' Isaac took the knife from him. He felt the heft of it in his hand, the tempered and riveted steel. He looked at the others. They were to be bound. They were to be a fellowship. He touched the bole of the lime tree next to him. He put the blade of the knife to it and began to carve, the cut bark falling away letter after carved letter, the trees seeming to press in around the three boys, the forest they were sworn to, their names carved on the tree, the word Brethren carved after them even though Wesley said that it was sacrilege.

'The Minister talked to you too, Wesley.'

'I didn't say otherwise, did I?' Wesley said.

'What did he say, Wesley?' Lynch said.

'He didn't say nothing is any of your business.'

'I know you, Wesley Upritchard. What did the Minister tell you?'

'He told you that you would be Minister after him, isn't that right?' Corry said.

Shepton Mallet
25th January 1945

'You did nothing with her in the picture house?' Davis said. Hooper towelling himself off in the shower. Two MPs outside the door.

'You wouldn't never believe me. Nobody else does.'

'And you says you never got a charver off her. Never got the tit, never mind the bush.'

'Stop that talk. She wasn't that kind of girl.'

'They never are. You reckon the MPs put them things in the locker?'

'They must of.'

'Why though?'

'When you're a black man you don't have to wonder about no why.'

'That's what you keep saying.'

'Listen, Davis, if me and you's going to escape, we better do it soon.'

'I haven't right worked out a plan yet.'

'You want this soap?'

'What do I want soap for?'

'You told me. You press a key into the soap then you can use the shape to make a skeleton key.'

'I got to go,' Davis said. 'Them MPs be coming for you any minute.'

*

'I got to talk to him in the bathhouse after the first day,' Davis told the men in the dining hall. 'He says he never done it but where did he get them ladies' things? They weren't took off no washing line. Has some notion about copying a key with a bar of soap.

'I could spring him,' Davis said, 'but I'm not going to

spring a guilty man, am I? Him and his simpleton talk of skeleton keys. How far would a black man get in this country anyhow?'

The other men knowing what was happening. Davis a blowhard, denial a currency in a place like this, bad intentions traded one to the other.

'Reckon you could break one of us out instead, Davis?' one of the men said.

'Maybe you could just spring yourself.'

'That would be admitting guilt,' Davis said, 'and I'm innocent of any crime and will state that in front of any court in the nation.'

*

'The evidence of the ladies' clothing was very damaging,' Phair said.

That's not damaging, getting pulled by your neck by a hangman's rope is damaging, Hooper thought, but he didn't say it. Hooper played dumb with Phair now. There was no point. There was a part you got to play in official rooms. The offices and waiting rooms and interview rooms with some cop looking at you over the top of a gunmetal typewriter and calling you boy. You got to be the downcast Negro. Knowing you done wrong. Having nothing to say for yourself, giving them sullen looks.

'I'm looking at mitigation here and I'm not seeing it. Your trespass at the airfield in Atlanta. Your work with the cameras in the Bomb Loft. The record says unauthorised access. Damage to a canvas-type floor covering.'

'It was only footprints.'

'It's the way it looks to the court.'

'Footprints to a dance.' Hooper said her name to himself, the inwards sound of it. Elspeth.

'That and your insistence that you attended the cinema with Miss Davidson.'

'I did, Sir.'

Morne
13th December 1944

Standing in the cinema foyer. Betty Grable in the 'Coming Attractions' case. Walking Liberty in his pocket, rubbing it between his thumb and forefinger for luck. Servicemen and their girls going in. Airmen with forage caps under an epaulette, the girls in crepe dresses, skirts with box pleats, stocking seams drawn on their calves with eyeliner. He saw Elspeth through the glass door, wearing a camel coat, a hat tilted to one side so that it hid her face, her look of wartime jeopardy, behind enemy lines in occupied territory, the espionage that is left to the heart.

She crossed the foyer and bought a ticket at the kiosk. She handed over the ticket at the door, the foyer emptying out. He gave her a moment then crossed to the doorway and went in. The newsreel running, flickering armies on the march. The names of distant places he never thought he would hear spoken, smoke hanging in the projector beams, men and women shifting and settling, thighs grazing. He stood in the curtained doorway, not knowing where to look for her. A hand took his.

'Come on. Margaret came in earlier. Her and her man are keeping seats for us.' Inching down the aisle, keeping their heads down. These were the double seats against the back wall and Hooper's legs brushed against the knees of couples. Aware of fondlings, trying to find gaps in clothing, the softness of things worn next to the skin, hems slipping up, blouses unbuttoned. A girl gasped in the dark as though something had been told to her, an act described, something she had never envisaged.

'Anything goes up here,' Margaret said. The young airman beside her got up and moved past Hooper. His face was turned away. Hooper saw the nape of his neck, blond hair cut to regulation length. Elspeth had told him she had never seen his face. There was a feeling of someone falling away from you, knowing that he had no part of this, mediums of altitude and cloud where he belonged. Margaret said that was why she never introduced the pilot to Elspeth. There was something airy and faraway about him. She got out of the seat. 'Was like the siege of Stalingrad keeping people out of this one.' Margaret giving them a sly look as they sat into the double seat.

'Keep your hands to yourself, soldier,' she said to Hooper, 'that there is the preacher's daughter.' Margaret knew what was said about the daughters of the cloth. That they would know more of sin than others. That they could reveal themselves concupiscent if they could be persuaded to it.

'He knows who I am, Margaret, thank you,' Elspeth said.

'Make sure he does. Me and Flight Officer Strain going to take a walk on the Avenue.'

'Least we know his name now. You're cracked on him, Margaret.'

'I am. He wants to marry me.'

'Oh, Margaret.'

'I know. You young people enjoy yourselves.'

Margaret made her way along the row of couples. If they noticed her passing they gave no sign.

'Margaret's the best,' Elspeth said, 'though she doesn't know when to stop talking.' Hooper wanted to say something but she put her finger to her lips and pointed to the screen where the film was starting. Lady in the Dark. He tried not to think that she was gaming with him. She was good at leaving things hanging in the air. She trailed half-grasped intentions behind her. She had taken his hand to lead him to the seat but he could not remember when she had let it go. She shifted in her seat so that the box pleats of her skirt rustled. You wonder do women mean these things.

She seemed so intent on the film that there might be nothing else in this world, sitting with her hands in her lap, palms up as if she might catch something falling from the plumed air above them.

The girl sitting to his right sighed, then went quiet. In the stalls far below them people smoked and made remarks. Sometimes someone laughed.

'Do you think he'll kiss her?' Elspeth said.

'What?'

'Do you think he'll kiss the girl before the end of the film?'

'I don't know. I'd say she don't. He's as dry as they come.'

'You want to bet?'

'Bet? Maybe. I got no money.'

'Nothing?'

'I got this.'

'What is it?'

'A silver half-dollar.'

'Let me.'

He held it in the air out of her reach.

'What's your bet?'

'Mine? I don't have any money either.'

'Well then.' He put the Walking Liberty back into his pocket. 'There's no bet is there?'

'What about a forfeit?'

'What kind of a forfeit?'

She didn't speak. The screen darkened for a night scene. Her hand almost unseen as she reached, only the white crescent of her nail as she put the tip of her index finger on the material of his trousers above the silver and put a small pressure on it so that it pushed into his thigh and held it for a moment before placing her hand back in her lap.

'Is that a deal?' he said. His voice thick.

'Yes. A minister's daughter's word is her bond.'

'Prove it,' he said.

'How do I do that?'

'Write it down.'

'You write it down. You can read and write, can't you?'

'Course I can. Keep your voice down.'

'I don't think anyone's worrying too much about us.'

'Write it down.'

'I haven't got a pen. Wait.'

'Wait for what?'

'Give me the coin. Just for a minute.'

Shepton Mallet
27th January 1945

Prosecutor's summation to the Court Martial of Private Gabriel Hooper

There are two dimensions to the case against the defendant Hooper. The first is the overwhelming body of evidence against the defendant. The second is the paucity of the evidence that he has been able to adduce in his defence. It is beyond dispute that Hooper met Miss Davidson at the dance in Warrenpoint on the night of 9th December. Hooper maintains that he danced with Miss Davidson, but if one leaves aside the fact that it is most unlikely that a clergyman's daughter would engage in the lascivious gyrations of the dance known as the 'Vogue' with a man of colour previously unknown to her, the defendant has been unable to produce any eye witness testimony to verify his assertion. And in fact his evidence has been wholly refuted by that of Miss Davidson's companion, Miss Reilly.

In the second instance Private Hooper is equally bereft of evidence of a supporting nature. He testifies that he attended the cinema with Miss Davidson yet no one saw her there. He tells the court that she entered furtively as some creature of the night may, as if he had not already traduced her body, he must also besmirch her reputation. In turn the cinema owner tells us by deposition that a Negro was seen lurking in the cinema foyer some time after the performance had begun but disappeared from view shortly afterwards. No doubt to prepare his assault on Miss Davidson. The victim's deposition executed by her father states that she had been engaged in serving light refreshments to the troops. Not by attending a film of dubious character in a less than glamorous provincial cinema.

Captain Phair's contention that a lovers' tryst had taken place in the cinema and that afterwards Miss Davidson had walked home alone has to be treated with the utmost circumspection. Captain Phair is entitled to defend his client, but the court martial is not to be taken as another dupe of this most feral man who stands accused before you. The proof of the baseness of his appetites has been arrayed on the evidence table during the course of these proceedings: these underthings belonging to the blameless creature Miss Davidson, this intimate apparel concealed in Hooper's locker, testified by the Reverend Davidson to be the possessions of his daughter. It was not enough that she be outraged but that she be further defiled by souvenir-taking of the basest kind.

I will not detain the court further. The defendant's case does not merit further consideration. It is as clear-cut an issue as can be imagined. Private Hooper waylaid a respectable young girl in a lonely spot at night and there unable to contain his animalistic urges, dishonoured her. We can only imagine her agitation of mind, and that of her father whose rightful protection of his daughter had failed through no fault of his own.

It is not for me to instruct the court martial as to its conclusions but right-thinking men must bear this in mind. That this war will come to an end. Many decent servicemen will have given their lives in pursuit of noble causes. While they were falling for their country an animal was gorging himself on another's innocence. And if he were to seek release from lawful custody in the years to come, would not our countrymen consider that we had not done our duty by permitting such a peril to our womenfolk to be allowed to roam free? I lay this before you for your consideration, confident that you will do your duty as have the many fallen of our countrymen.

Nineteen

Reay said the Nissen hut on the aerodrome was her favourite place on earth. Given a choice, she said, she'd live there for ever. The door faced south and she would sit with her back to the sun-warmed planks facing the sea, her eyes closed. Harper cleaned out the stove and he lit it for them on dark evenings, the wind blustery, the sand hissing on the runway concrete, shorelines on the move bringing shell fragments, empty anemone casings, hollowed-out crab bodies, sea gleanings blown past the tin walls. The hut had been stripped of all but lockers and bedframes, the springs rusted and detached. Stay away from them things, Ghost, Harper told Cole, you'll get tetanus off them.

Harper and Reay said they would have a house by the sea when they got away from the home. Reay said she wanted to lie on the dry sand in the shelter of dunes watching the little hairs on her arms turned blonde in the sun, sand grains caught in them. Harper said he wanted to be on the beach in wintertime, bundled up against the offshore wind, making fires of driftwood on the ocean margin, both taken with nostalgia for things that had never happened, homecomings, fire-lit interiors.

In the last warm days of summer Cole saw that she was pregnant. He didn't ask any more. Reared in the town estates it was enough that Harper and Reay took what they could in life, for nothing more was offered save what came from themselves, and everything relayed to the heart was improvised and temporary. The wind that blew down the Avenue where couples went on a Saturday night, the sound of seaspray on the Esplanade shelters, the rustle of awkward caresses. These sounds amounted to all the avowal they needed.

Reay wanted someone to read to her. Cole found a book called Horseman of the King in one of the lockers, which was the story of John Wesley. He read to her about John Wesley's early years and how he had been plucked from a house fire so that he made his escape with hardly a second to spare.

There were other books in the series. The Story of Helen Keller or The Story of Florence Nightingale. Reay made him promise that he would come to their house on the beach and read to the child.

Reay started to wear loose clothes when she was in the home. Cheesecloth blouses and gypsy skirts, the stylised troubadour fashions of the time. She made trouble with the other girls in the shower room so that she could shower on her own, although the other girls knew what was happening. They knew she went into the dormitory toilet cubicle in the morning, leaned her head against the verdigrised pipework and vomited, the knowledge of her pregnancy dormitory contraband, some girls wanting to sit on her bed and share secrets, but Reay was known to lash out. Gang culture had followed them into the home. You had to be careful where you went on your own. Alliances formed based on streets, on dress codes, on undercurrents of past delinquency that none of them could put a name to but that they saw in each other's eyes.

Harper and Reay were romanced in the home. They were seen as outlaws, paths of freedom and of conflict laid out in front of them. They were able to find the radical spaces in the home buildings. As if in an old photograph, eyes narrowed against the sun, casual, insolent. Harper had a way of lounging against things, smoking, a far-off drollery in his eyes. Something old-fashioned about him, something courtly. Reay the volatile one. You didn't get on the wrong side of her, but she was given to sentiment. The younger girls brought her drawings and woodblocks from the woodwork class with hearts burned into the grain and she lined the windowsill behind her bed with them. She cut articles from magazines and newspapers about mothers and daughters reunited after long separation. There was television in the games room between seven and eight each evening. They watched Coronation Street and Crossroads. The others could hear Reay crying during the sad parts.

'You would cry if you were me,' she said. Nobody answered. Nobody knew much about where Reay came from. Some post-war flats complex. Lives ground down. Concrete walkways and urine-smelling lift shafts. Feeling small in the towers and worn-out shopping plazas, austere and loveless townscapes, dismay pooling in people's hearts. Love a commodity. It had to be eked out. There wasn't enough to go around.

They knew Reay was good at taking things. Cutlery from the canteen, staplers, cigarette lighters and pens belonging to staff members. Klepto, she called herself. She had the tradecraft of palming things, of concealment, of remote looks that carried you beyond the moment, the street thief's toolkit. Her locker searched by staff every few weeks, her bedding thrown on the floor and the mattress flipped over. There was a sly side to her.

It got harder for Harper and Reay to see each other. Superintendent Upritchard put barriers in their way, introduced arbitrary rules, different meal times. Harper and Reay having to come up with elaborate stratagems. The building starting to take on the feel of a prisoner of war camp. Harper and Reay met in the boiler room, set out on elaborate journeys at pre-determined times. Notes written on cigarette papers were slipped between them. Cole was a courier. The ghost. He was good at getting past adults, not making eye contact. Slipping through enemy lines with messages then keeping guard as Harper and Reay went at each other. Draining clinches, teenage kisses like being bitten, mouths locked on, somehow including him in it with murmurings, escaped sighs, an erotic succour in the back stairs and boiler houses and dusty storerooms.

'When I get out of here I'm going to come back for thon Upritchard bastard,' Harper said.

'Never mind him. As long as you come back for me. Us.' Reay touched her belly and put her hand on the boy's shoulder.

'I'm coming back,' Harper said. Harper and Reay knowing what was at stake, how they were seen by the other residents. They could feel the waves of longing coming towards them, the welling up of the unloved.

Harper was coming up for discharge. There was a hearing. Don't be fighting with them, Reay said. This was time for contrite looks, shoulders slumped as if in defeat. She fussed over him the night before. Brushed his hair back from his forehead. Got cross over the length of his fingernails, scolded him over his frayed shirt collar, backed away when he reached out for her, no roaming hands when something of such importance was afoot. She had a range of what she imagined a wife's role might be, a world of feigned dismays and homely concern. Of sending men out into the world. Of waiting for them to come home.

*

'Done the discharge board,' Harper said, 'got past it I think.' He stood up straight and put his hands down by his sides. 'Please I will be a good person. Please I will contribute to society. I will no longer be a juvenile delinquent.'

'Glad to hear it,' Reay said, 'I don't want to be wasting my time on a corner boy.' Wife parodies now. Arms folded under her breasts. Taking no nonsense. Harper acting the cowed husband, fake resentful, hangdog, looking up at her out of the corner of his eye.

'I'm going to write to you all the time,' Reay said. She would be discharged in six months. She put her hand on his chest, fingered the buttons on his shirt. The frontier wife, seeing herself in gingham, her husband going out on the trail. 'I'll find us all somewhere to live,' Harper said. There would be cooking smells from the kitchen. There would be decorous sex on clean-smelling linen sheets.

'You look after my girl for me,' Harper said. Cole sat on a radiator watching them, listening intently, thinking that maybe promises had to be heard in a certain way otherwise they would be broken. There was always a child's face pressed to the back window of a car being driven away from some lost household, adults left standing in the street looking after the car, downcast, a hierarchy of defeated looks, overcome by sadnesses of their own making. An adult's undertaking to be better next time, the hand not to be lifted, the food to be bought, the money not to be spent, the clothes to be washed, the baby not to cry but to be picked up and held. Ordinary falsehoods.

'We'll come back for you when you're old enough. You know how I know that? Because if it was the other way round, you'd come back for us.'

*

Discharge Board Hearing re Michael Anthony Harper, 12th October 1972

The applicant was successful. The board examined the applicant's history and concluded that he was in a position to make a contribution to society. That he had exhibited a willingness to reform. His disciplinary record at the Morne home was satisfactory although some minor infractions were reported.

HM Superintendent of the Morne home, Reverend Upritchard, stated that some aspects of the life of the home had been rendered difficult if not unmanageable by the presence of the applicant. Reverend Upritchard said that Harper was 'an incorrigible' but was extremely intelligent and well able to steer clear of trouble.

Sergeant Lynch said that in his experience young men like the applicant were likely to 'graduate' to adult prison. He also said that the home could become an 'academy of crime' and it were better that the younger residents were protected from the likes of the applicant.

Reverend Upritchard concurred and said that he would be glad to see the back of the applicant and that some others in the school could in his opinion be guided back to the 'straight and narrow'. In particular one girl who required corrective action of the most severe kind if she were not to adopt a 'life of crime'.

The chairman of the board, Magistrate Corry, thanked the members for their diligence. In the light of all submissions it was proposed that the applicant be granted parole on the usual conditions. Sergeant Lynch suggested the additional condition that the applicant be disbarred from coming within ten miles of the town and from having contact with any of the residents, and this proposal was adopted. The meeting concluded with a scripture reading from Reverend Upritchard.

*

Letter #2

Well my boy Mr Upritchard didn't waste no time coming after me after he got you off the premises he fetched up in the dormitory two hours after lights out he says it was a search for goods missing from the premises. As a thief in the night as he says himself him and Dr Eugene come into the dormitory in the middle of the night lights on girls crying etc etc I says to Upritchard if you're looking the ride there's easier ways of doing it and he says I'm a harlot which is a fancy slut and the worst thing to be in the world according to him standing there with the

189

eyes bulged out of his head he tosses the bed and the locker and there's nothing there to find so he says he's going to search my person I says you'll lay no hand on me you're not allowed but he says he has Dr Eugene there and he can be there so it'll be the two of you getting an eyeful then I says I thought I'd get a clip some of the girls are roaring crying and he says for them to quit their screeching he's always on about the Lord but there was no word of the Lord that night.

Upritchard and Eugene pulls me into the bathroom I was ready to throw myself out the window if one of them put a hand near my clothes I swear to God then the Matron walks in what do you think you're doing to that child she says I was never so glad to see anybody in my life. Upritchard starts on about the things I took the Matron she's got these slitty eyes on her I was glad she was looking at him not looking at me.

Can you not see she's expecting the Matron says well that stopped the two boys in their tracks you'd have to laugh at the look on their faces I thought Upritchard was going to start preaching now the whole world knew I was a harlot sprung from the loins of Satan he says loins my eye I says but the Matron turns the evil eye on me and says that's enough so I give her this meek look please Matron stay on my side for ever.

Get back into bed girls she says to the rest of them and off they go not a word out of them then I want to see you in the infirmary in the morning.

My demon lover (ha!) I seen the look Upritchard had in his eye and Eugene like the undead with his fat white hands the thought of them anywhere near me I seen the look and the sooner I get out of here the better I'll give this to the ghost to post for me and you just keep thinking babies' names.

Reay xxxxxooooo

The Lighthouse Cafe
27th November 2000

Upritchard dreamed of the girl in the pit. His surroundings
mocked him. The posters in dirty frames, men and women
frozen in mid-season gaiety. He lagged pipes with old jumpers
and pushed teatowels into the gaps between frame and
window. Rime frosted the inside of the single windowpanes,
starred and crystalline and aglitter when he turned his torch
on them so that they seemed their own nebulae, something
cold and far away. He sat alone by a paraffin stove in the
kitchen. There was a leather suitcase on the table in front of
him, the lid covered in yellowed travel labels for Skegness
and Brighton, the sea on shingle beaches, lights strung
along Victorian esplanades, pierside amusements. Long-
gone summers. The suitcase contained files that he had kept
from the home, concealed from Lynch and Corry. He kept
it hidden under his bed like something an adolescent would
conceal, smutty, lingered over.

The girls all have the look of runaways. Postered on police station noticeboards. The look worked at, the mouth pursed, the
shoulders hunched. Always just a little too much eyeliner. Lipstick always a shade too full, gone-off rosebud, the lips down-
turned at the corners. The hair always limp. It can't carry its own
weight. The eyes are full of choices not thought through, you
can read the years there, the reports following them around, the
tales of dark truancy, the vocabulary of lost girls. *Out of control.*
Promiscuous. The eyes said you can be let down more ways
than you can guess. In more places. There is always something
else to be taken away. The appetite for hurt goes unsated.

Reay's photograph had been taken when she arrived at the home in November 1971. She's looking straight at the camera, smiling, some wryness she'd picked up in her sinning, a defiant retort on her lips. Trailing a history of disruption behind her, school expulsions, alcohol consumption, truancy. *We'll have to keep an eye on this one.* He was not to know she was with child. The Matron's hand shaking him awake, an infant's cry in the top corridor. Eugene bent over her taking the pulse. The Matron weeping. *The first peace she's ever known.*

Upritchard went to the front of the cafe, looking down across the dunes to the caravan park. Kay's light on, Cole's car outside. None of the other caravans was occupied. He could make out the shapes of the caravans spread across the hardstanding as though a silent army had set up camp there, ghost bivouacs. A white envelope had been pushed under the door, the white paper unsullied against the sea grit and debris carried across the threshold.

He leaned down to lift the unmarked envelope. It contained one half of a photograph, torn across the middle. He recognised the boy, the smile that left his eyes aslant. The children of that time looking slum-bred, growth-stunted. The photograph itself getting under the surface of the image, finding the grave pallor of the time. As though the flesh itself had been different, more nuanced, prone to shadow.

The photograph had been torn diagonally so that you could see another boy's feet at the bottom of the image. Harper's left arm was raised as if it was around the other boy's shoulders. Upritchard knew what this kind of correspondence meant. Chain or poison pen letters, anonymous, unsigned. You pictured someone alone in a room, cutting and pasting, piecing it together with misspellings, repetitions. There would be scrapbooks, a corkboard with newspaper cuttings on it, pages covered in spidery handwriting.

He carried the photograph through to the kitchen and put it on the shelf above his desk, against the old till rolls, paid dockets and accounts fallen due. He picked up the phone and called the station. He told Lynch about the photograph.

'Do you think it got took out of Isaac's safe?'

'Could of done.'

'What do I do with it?'

'The photograph? Do what you want. The dead can't hurt nobody.'

'I wouldn't be so sure about that. The dead's wandering about this town looking for mischief to do. What we done to the black man years ago wasn't our fault. Minister told us it was the Lord's work. Nobody told us to do nothing with the girl Wilkinson. In that matter, Sergeant, we were forsaken of ourselves. Pride told us to take a name and we called ourselves Brethren.'

'Somebody is trying to spook you. Doing a good job of it.'

'I'm sat here looking at the face of death. And if that face had a tongue to tell it would say that somebody else knows about us.'

'Hold your peace, Upritchard. Knowing something and proving it is another thing.'

'Minister Davidson used to say you don't sit still and wait for the Lord to find you. You hunt him out or you will be hunted.'

'Or the devil.'

'He never said that. Are we to bury Isaac?'

'There has to be an inquest, I told you. And Isaac can't be coroner at his own inquest. He'll sit on ice until the autopsy. Someone will be appointed to do him and the girl.'

'When is that?'

'Who knows?'

Upritchard put the phone down on the counter. Above the counter was a monochrome photograph of workers from the construction of the aerodrome. They were looking across the runway with troubled expressions as though the building of it had uncovered a desolation in the landscape that no one had been aware of up until then.

The sandpit had been dug in the years after the war. Worked out and left, water gathering in the bottom, brackish from salt spray blown across the apron, wired off against strays, the wire slackening with the movement of the ground. The night Reay died they placed her body in the boot of Corry's car and drove it to the aerodrome. They took turns one after the other to carry the body to the side of the pit where they stood for a moment, three men, a nativity mocked, not Brethren of the light but of the dark.

*

In the police station Lynch rewound the street footage of the night Corry died. A strange, over-exposed night scene, light flaring from the top right-hand corner, everybody looking stealthy and achromatic. The feeling that a crime is taking place somewhere just out of shot. A feeling that you are witnessing someone's last moments. He placed it with stills of hooded youths vaulting shop counters, a homemade weapon in hand. The juddery rewind. The uneven tape speed. The streets deserted. The wind blew up from the sea along the rising streets and lifted ice particles from the roadway, so you imagined you could hear the hiss of them, feel the fine abrading along windowsills and handrails.

Lynch wondered if he knew the town any more. People's behaviour was changing. They seemed aware of being continually filmed, cameras on the street and inside shops, dramatic texture being added to their lives, being tracked across the retail space, hurrying across the sightlines. In the camera murk everyone looking suspect, shadowed. There was a harried, last-minute air.

Lynch thinks he's been doing this job too long. How many years since the CCTV came in and does anyone else think those years with a joystick between your finger and thumb are long enough? Zoom, freeze, rewind. You wouldn't believe what came off the ferry now. Eastern Europeans. Asylum seekers. Prostitutes from countries you couldn't even pronounce. Bartered. Trafficked. These are haunted roads. Sometimes he's afraid to even look at them. Sometimes he can't sleep at night.

He sees a figure come out the bottom of Hospital Street, bent forward against the ice-sting. Hard to make out if it was a man or woman, the night kept throwing up light anomalies, flare spots from the blown ice, streetlights flaring downward. The figure turned right, towards Sandmarl Street, keeping close to the wall, bundled, furtive. Holding a bag close like something long hoarded.

The tapes have looped the same scene over and over, the

195

tape heads dirty, the emulsion degraded so you see things and don't see them at the same time. There seem to be afterimages, night-time scenes which seem to belong to different places, haunted towns from other eras. The tape speed wrong so that the ghost people are moving at silent-era speed, jerky, semi-comic. Snatches from the archive, noiseless and flickering.

Lynch loses the person he is tracking. The street is empty but there's a bag against the library door.

Lynch kept a camp bed in his office. He dozed on it in the evening. At nightfall he rose to sit at the bank of cameras again. The exterior cameras were partly frozen over, the lenses bordered with ice. The wind had turned some of them on their brackets so that they were focused on rooftops, down into the back yards of the town. The technology was old, the cameras needing cleaned. The recorders behind him whirred, tape slapping through the spindles. The phone rang.

'Lorna Annett, Sergeant.'

'What is it?'

'Dr Eugene's not in his bed. Took some clothes from the staffroom.'

'Did you look in the grounds?'

'We looked. Nobody seen him.'

'I'll look on the CCTV, but if he was on the street I would have seen him.'

'He could freeze out there in the night.'

'I'll look again.' *Do us all a favour if he froze.* A figure moving on the camera at the Harbour Road junction, walking towards the harbour. Eugene. Lynch put on his coat.

They think Eugene sleeps but he does not. Memories of war keep him awake. He has seen subs moored at Holywell, the streaked plating, the stressed hull vaned and streamlined. In the hospital he dreams of his end. He dreams of ghost wolf packs hunting in the frozen northern seas. Under the ice pack.

Lieutenant Francis Eugene, late of Halifax, England, is absent without leave from the Morne hospital complex. There are duties he wishes to attend to. There are debts he wished to address. He had been medical officer to RN V-class destroyer Dunedin. Cruising in convoy three hundred and twenty nautical miles north-west of Archangel on convoy escort. Travelling at fourteen knots in a heavy swell. Her ironbound hull, keel laid in Portsmouth shipyard in 1941. The salt spray froze as it landed on stanchions and handrails and men were sent aloft to chip it from radio arrays and mastheads. Gannets and black-headed gulls followed in her wake.

The convoy was attacked at 04.00. It was attacked again at 07.25. Further attacks were mounted on the approaches to Archangel. He remembered bunker oil alight in the water. Bilge leachates. Early in the morning they steamed into the aftermath of a sinking, tarry corpses adrift in the frozen waters, floating in circles, a dawn patrol of the damned. Gouts of foul air vented from sunk ships carrying with them burnt debris, clothing and charred papers. There were burning ships, the air full of fumes. Tankers of ship's crude and aviation kerosene burned all that day and the next night and would not be doused. The destroyer sailed back and forwards through the fumes and the men coughed and spat and their eyes streamed and the fumes would part from time to time to display an occult scene, the dead afloat among the scorched and broken masts of merchantmen.

Lieutenant Eugene's discharge papers stated that he was suffering from nervous exhaustion. For some years after the war he became an itinerant doctor, working in small hospitals in far-flung towns. In 1961 he was censured by the medical council for writing methadone scripts. Restrictions were placed on his licence to practise. In 1966 he was arraigned at Southwark Crown Court on a charge of procuring abortions but the main police witness failed to appear and the charges were dropped. In 1970 he was employed as medical officer to the Morne home and was retained there until its closure.

*

Lynch walked out onto the pier. At nightfall the rain had turned to ice on the bare concrete so that he could hear the sound of the frost under his boots. The frozen pier looked like an ingot of white light laid into the darkness of the sea. There was no other sound save his boots on the frost. The tide was high. The water smoked, tendrils of cold air adrift over the pier edge and the inset iron bollards. The crane gantries stood as wayposts the length of the white walkway.

As he reached the pier light a trawler came around the navigation light. A ghost boat he thought it at first. The water barely stirred at her forefoot. The way was off her and the water barely stirred at her forefoot. The seabed was littered with hulks and she looked like one of them raised. Three men stood on the deck wearing oilskins and rigger boots. They neither looked his way nor lifted a hand to acknowledge him. They had the eyes of drowned men the sea had returned. Lynch let them pass. He had his own dead to attend to.

The gates of the container yard were open. Lynch went through. The stevedores had withdrawn labour for the night. There were reports of frozen winches, falls on iced-over gantry platforms, metal gone brittle in the cold. The ferry would not dock until late morning.

The containers were lined and stacked four high with a runway between them. The runways had been left in shadow all day. The low sun had not reached them. The metal walls contracting in the cold creaked like pack ice. A shadow crossed the end of one of the container avenues, stopped for a moment – *follow me* – and then went on.

Lynch went through the main gate. He looked for footprints on the pier wall and on the quayside leading towards the graving dock but he could see nothing. Plaques of ice broken from the pier wall chinked against the armour stones of the pier and as he looked towards the sound he saw movement on the bridge of the grounded trawler. Through her broken wheelhouse windows he saw someone standing on the bridge, a shadowy helmsman. Lynch slid down the pier wall and climbed over the rock armour to reach the half-sunk prow of the boat. He took hold of the gunwale and pulled himself onto her deck. The wheelhouse windows were empty. He climbed the metal ladder on the side of the wheelhouse and tried the wheelhouse door. The latch housing was rusted and the lock turned slowly. In the distance he heard the deck klaxon of a freighter as it rounded the Mew Island light. He put his weight against the latch bar to swing the metal door inwards.

From the dockside Eugene watching Lynch enter the wheelhouse then he began to walk back towards the town. The Matron would know of his night's doings.

Lynch stepped into the wheelhouse. The fittings had been salvaged, the wheel and instruments gone. Wiring looms hung from the ceiling covered in hoar frost. The gangway to the sunken crew quarters filled with a square of black water. There was a black plastic bag on the dented instrument console. Lynch emptied it out onto the floor. He reached down for the first object, not recognising it at first, the flimsy pencil straps, the satin of it water-stained, the lace edging frayed. The names running through his head from catalogues of long ago. Cami. Sheer. A silk belt, the little buckles, the material yellowed with age. The silk stockings pooled on the floor. He thought of them as they once were, scented, flimsy, the black seam taut against the calf, not seen since he had placed them in the Negro soldier's locker.

Standing up, he brushed against the wiring and ice flakes fell on his face like sleet and he stood expressionless as though imagined winters of his youth blew through his mind. The wash of the freighter he had heard struck the side of the Brighter Morn and the deck rolled under his feet.

Twenty

Morne
27th November 2000

The girl's body waits in the morgue. Catacombed. The room is unquiet. From time to time the undertaker Morgan visits it to check the temperature of the cabinets. There's a flickering fluorescent light that he means to fix. Damp glistens on the walls. He feels bunkered, as if he is in a survivalist zone, a place of faltering civilisations. It's easy to believe that things have fallen apart outside and that he alone is left. He has been told to check the autopsy instruments, the bone saws. The callipers and retractors.

Corry's body is in an adjacent cabinet. Death makes companions of strange folk, Morgan said. Mind, nobody's in any rush to bury him. I haven't had instructions from the wife yet. Do you think he was pushed, his assistant said. There wouldn't be too many crying if he was, Morgan said.

Cole had said he would meet Kay at the pool. He helped her to break up the surface ice using a pole with a net hoop on the end, the net long rotted. When she came out of the changing cubicle he watched her walk to the edge of the pool. He thought about lovers she might have had, first touches in darkened bedrooms, parents downstairs, fending a boy off with small chaste gestures. A bookish girl, earnest. She would be a librarian when she grew up.

'You see enough?' she said.

'Sorry.'

'I been stared at too much in this pool.' She dived from the pool rail and stayed under, surfacing at the far end of the pool at a distance from the harbour lights so that he could only make out the pale arrows of her shoulders. She turned and swam lengths freestyle with goggles and cap, pushing water in front of her, breathing on the upstroke, her exhalations coming back off the poolside tiling, swimming like a 1950s Olympian, a girl from an industrial town in Eastern Europe, the daughter of a steelworker.

She pulled herself onto the poolside. He put her worn towel around her shoulders, rubbing the coarse fibres into her skin. He could feel the chill through the material.

'You need to get dressed.'

'He says.'

'Where did you learn to swim?'

'I did athletics. I swam in competitions. I used to get up at five in the morning. I would look out the window and Dad would be waiting for me in his van. He'd drive me to the pool in the dark. He never said a word. When I got out he would take me to school. He worked on the ships.'

Cole could see how these might be the fathering hours. The lost times before dawn when nothing else was abroad. A rusted and scarred van parked in the corner of the swimming pool asphalt.

'I liked organising things. Colour-coding socks in the

drawer. I sorted his toolbox for him. They couldn't have any more children. I had posters of Mark Spitz and Johnny Weissmuller on my bedroom wall.'

An only child. They'd lie awake at night listening to her breathing. Her father getting out of bed and crossing the landing to make sure, padding across the carpet. A child born late in life. They thought they had travelled beyond such largesse. You had to hold your breath. The distances between you seemed so great. Lying awake, heartstruck. Spitz and Weissmuller. Olympians, legends appointed to guard her when she slept.

'I never got to wear jeans or trainers. They used to put me in little dresses, pigtails in my hair tied up with ribbons. My mother would comb my hair for hours in front of the mirror.' Her father sitting at the table watching them, big-boned and awkward. She was tiny, out-of-date. She carried little patent leather handbags. Other girls said cruel things. Her parents' names were Sandra and Kenny. They were like people who had seen a film of parenthood a long time ago and had tried to recreate it from memory. Whole passages were missing. No one knew what came next.

Sandra at her dressing table. Yellow puckers in the varnish. Sandra would light a cigarette and leave it poised on the edge. Kay following it all, the little inner gestures, the pursing, the dabbing with tissue. Working your way towards the innermost self. That was what all the little mirrored cases were about, the brushes and pencils, the clasps and trinketry.

Kenny would record everything on a super eight camera, swimming regattas, family excursions, trips to the amusements, trips to the beach. He was at home with the mechanics of things. Sandra sat at the back of the seating area, knitting. She never lifted her head, even when Kay was swimming. They were grateful that she was there, making her way to the diving board, barefoot, lithe, padding across the runner matting.

They drove past the Avenue in Kay's car. The winter Avenue. The trees leafless. Two hundred years ago there was an abbey at the end of the Avenue but it was burned and its stones are overgrown. Unquiet memory stirs in the undergrowth of the holly trees and lime trees that line the Avenue. Kay stopped the car at the entrance.

'They come up here when the bars close,' Kay said.

'For what?'

'What do you think? Girls and boys. After the bars, after the pictures.'

'Looks like a place you'd find a body. We need to talk.'

'You don't come to the Avenue for talking.'

'What do you come for?'

She leaned towards him. He felt the light, dry touch of her lips.

'Forward. My mother's word. Am I forward?' She held herself against him, weighted, pressed into him, given.

She let go and got out of the car. She walked to the entrance to the Avenue, stood there framed by the gate pillars. He took her hand. They were in a place of allowed touches. A quick feel through clothing, on top of underthings. The withheld world had its protocols.

'Was there a place like this where you came from? We had one. The back of the prefabs at school.' As if every town had its shadowed places of encounter, dead-end alleys, old buildings, tree-lined river walks, and there was an instinct to them, an erotic largesse of place, where the town dreamed of itself in the bodies of its adolescents, of forbidden touches, faltering handholds.

'There was a cinema,' he said.

'A picture house. The back seats where nobody could look down on you?'

'Yes.'

'And girls?'

'Yes.'

'They have names, these girls?'

'We never asked their names.'

'I should have known. What was the cinema like?'

'Old-fashioned. People used to throw cigarettes from the balcony into the stalls.' Ushers with torches. Velvet seats worn to the nap. Comet tails in the dark.

'Did it have a name, this picture house?'

'The Vogue.'

She backed him up against a tree. He wondered if she thought he was someone else. He felt as if he was a sequence of fondling and holding. That this night was something she held in earnest. How she traced his lips with her forefinger. There was a choreography to be observed. The way she allowed him to slip his hand through an opening in her parka, the tempos and repositionings, the way her own hand moved under his shirt, found bare skin. Putting his hand between her legs. She brought something courtly and nuanced to the night, to the lewd touchings. He felt her attention move away from him.

'What is it?'

She pointed. Behind his head the word *Brethren* inscribed into the tree, the bark grown out around it.

'The Brethren?'

'The Elected Brethren. The tin hut church they all belong to.'

'Doesn't seem like their kind of place. Up here. At this time of night. It's been here for a while, years by the look of it. Names underneath. I can't make them out.'

'Let me see.' She traced the words with her fingers.

Isaac Corry

Wesley Upritchard

John Lynch

15 Dec 1944

'I know these names,' she said.

'What were they up to?'

'I don't know.'

A single word underneath the names. Brethren.

'I want to go home,' she said.

He sat at the caravan window, looking north, and waited for Kay to come back from Lily. Wind had scoured away the runway markings. Anything not made of concrete or stone had been eroded by salt and the north-east wind, the corroded stumps of building frames sunk in the runway margins. The caravan park set down on the aircraft hardstandings, the caravans sparsely lit with an air of marginal settlement, their aluminium cladding salt-pitted.

Powder snow blew in from the sea and turned in the wind

as though it attached itself to shapes that danced unseen and sported on the runway. The foghorn on the Haulbowline lighthouse sounded and the brass bell on the Opal shallows rang dull and cracked three miles away, call and return, night given voice. He heard her come in.

'How was Lily?'

'Working on her shroud, poor thing.'

'Her shroud?'

'The Brethren. The women start to make their own shroud when they're fourteen to remind them about mortality.'

'Was Lily ever married?'

'No. But she can't remember if she was or not. She hides her sewing every time I come into the house. Not the only one hides things around here.'

'Tell me more about your family.'

'Why should I?'

'Because I didn't have one.'

'Where do I start?'

'You have photographs?'

She showed him a monochrome photograph taken just after her parents married. Her father burly, authoritative, wearing an evening suit and black tie, hair Brylcreemed back from his forehead. He was smoking a cigarette. He looked capable of violence, a back-street enforcer with a lethal swagger. She didn't recognise the background. The West End of a city somewhere, cruel and vibrant, men with cold eyes in well-cut suits, the women's mouths looking like their faces had been slashed with open razors. Her mother wore her hair up in a French bun, her eyes heavy with mascara, dark lipstick, her waist nipped in. This was the couple who should

have had a child, not the lost parents she remembered. This
street mother would have been different, reeking of gin, spite-
ful, directing cutting remarks. There would have been fights,
slammed doors. As a child she said she worried that these parents were in the house somewhere. That another hard-bitten
life awaited her.

When the house was empty she would go into the bathroom and take down her father's cologne and smell it, a mas-
culine odour under the sweet tones, a lowlife rankness.

She talked into the night in the gas-jet hiss of the Superser,
the caravan close and airless, the whorled intimacies examined, Kay a tender-hearted rationalist. She talked and did
not ask him about himself. Reticence must be allowed its
moment. There was space in her life for the close of heart.
Her father spoke little and she knew how silence worked. Her
mother showed her how to operate within the confines of a
man's silence. Whole days would go past without anything
being said. He would have been better off in an order of con-
templatives, his quiet become a rich, monkish thing, and it
made her easy in the realm of the untold.

'It's like a film,' she said.

'What is?'

'You. A stranger comes to town. All of a sudden things start
to happen.'

'Things happen anyway.'

'You fit the character though.' A man who sat at her fold-
down table, laconic, burdened.

'I just want to fulfil my client's requirements and get out
of here.'

'How do you do that?'

'Identify the body.'

'How? You got DNA, forensics?' She liked the tech words, the way things could be broken down, codes retrieved, recreated under lab conditions. Authorities would be involved, serious people in white coats. You could defer to them. We were all made of the same things, differently ordered. We were all dust blown across the universe in cosmic gales. You could gaze upon what was eternal in your bones, the star matter, the icy filigree of self.

'There's nobody to compare it against. No DNA samples. Anyway, it's not the kind of proof the client is looking for.'

'What then?'

'Her clothes. I know what she would have been wearing.'

'Where are they?'

'They'll be at the morgue.'

'There's more to it.'

'What makes you think that?'

'There always is.'

When he was in the shower Kay opened his briefcase, thumbing back the brass clasp. She felt hunched-over, thievish, looking back over her shoulder, dry-mouthed. The briefcase interior smelt of leather and copying fluid. There were photocopies of land registry documents. She opened them out, trying to keep them in the correct folds. Things had to be returned to the case in the right sequence. The banquette light cast her shadow against the wall, a crabbed, underhand figure. She put the legal documents aside. There was a dental record in the name of Reay Wilkinson. Police reports on absconded teenagers, press cuttings from local papers, the pages yellowed, brittle along the folds where they had been opened out, reeking of harm. They looked like scattered documents retrieved after a catastrophe. Copies of statements and court documents. Committal orders. Documents rendered illegible by damp stains. An envelope containing photographs.

They'd photographed themselves in a place Kay didn't recognise, a planked interior, utilitarian materials, an old single bedstead with a blanket thrown over it, a pot-bellied stove. Polaroids, the colours otherworldly, the emulsions fading, red-eye giving the older boy a feral look, the girl acting tough, glaring at the camera so that you wondered what outlaw world she imagined herself in, what on-the-run interlude, death's agents on the trail, what flinty-eyed G-men of her imagination. Cole stood to one side, unposed, not looking at the camera, hands in his pockets.

In the side pocket of the briefcase there was a blue envelope with a single sheet of paper in it, the paper watermarked Basildon Bond which made her think of letters from another era, close-written intimacies. The envelope was addressed John Cole Solicitor, c/o Tayside Courts. She opened the letter. 'Body found on Pirnmill aerodrome. May be Reay Wilkinson.' Signed 'A Well-wisher'. The writing crabbed, seeming worked at under a dim light. The signature full of threat, other agendas, indiscernible malice. *A Well-wisher.*

There were more photographs, taken outside. Kay thinks she can place them by the shape of the mountains behind them, somewhere on the western edges of the aerodrome. Harper and Reay are paddling. Reay's wearing a cheesecloth shirt and has her hippy skirt bunched, holding it up in one hand. He has his trousers rolled up and a handkerchief folded over his head. They're a parody couple, industrial workers on an annual jaunt to a seaside of donkey rides and kiss-me-quick hats. She's acting a knock-kneed matron and he's a banty little trade unionist. The sun glints on the waves behind them, what might pass for happiness in burnished glimpses. She imagined buckets and spades, candy-striped deckchairs, the heatstruck ephemera of a day at the seaside. The boy taking the photographs happiest when he's just out of frame, a figure at the edge of the crowd.

In the bottom of the case there was a hardback copy of Horseman of the King, The Story of John Wesley. The dust jacket faded and torn, the red cloth binding showing through. She wondered if this was how Cole saw himself, a carrier of the flame, a man with a staff set out on the road, burdened, carrying light into the pilgrim dark.

She opened the book. Ran her eye over words of duty and of reprimand. Under the flyleaf an old aerogramme, franked USAAF mail service, a censor's stamp on the exterior.

Pte Gabriel Hooper, Pirnmill Airbase

Dear Gabriel I am glad you are down in Europe the sea is wide and there are many dangers therein. I prayed for He Commandeth and Raiseth the Stormy Wind, which Lifteth up the Waves Thereof. Nothing changed here. The foundry is busy with the war I trust this letter will not find you in liquor or in disgrace for there is much of that here none of it good. I never wanted for you to enlist but now you done it you make the best of it but working in a movie theater over there when you could have stayed here and done the same thing

still you get three meals a day and maybe stay out of them places
where Dwell the Violent Against Man and Blasphemers of God. Like
your mother you long to dance and look where that got her. Never
mind that path is barren now and I will not talk of it. They will not
let a boy such as you go to be a pilot you know that and I rejoice for
I cannot bear the idea of a boy being put on high where you used to
fear the lightning would set the clouds afire. The little boy who shelled
peas with me and come to my bed ashiver for it was thundering
outside is gone to manhood now but I remember.

    Yr grandmother
    Ellie Hooper

The blue paper of the aerogramme fashioned to travel through an ethereal place, rarefied atmospheres, the empty spaces above the cloud, blown about by wind currents. The words could not come back unchanged. She put the aerogramme and the letter back in the book and closed the briefcase.

When he came out of the shower she got up to go to bed. She wiped the table and placed their cups in the sink. She pulled the collar of her dressing gown up around her neck and tied her hair into a ponytail then took off her make-up at the mirror over the sink. She kissed him closemouthed on the lips. The light, sour touch of her lips like sweat drying between the shoulder blades. As far as you get tonight.

He sat at the couchette after she went to bed. He took an Ordnance Survey map of the town from his briefcase. The topography, the aerodrome and the township around the old harbour that had been erased to build it. There were contours there that could not be seen, the shoreline constantly changing, sandbanks washed away in storms, dunes blown across the aerodrome. The ground underneath the runways unreliable. New housing had been built across the northern reaches of the town. The principal features of the town were named on the map, the churches, the hospital, bridges and fords, the tracework of place. The Avenue, the Bomb Loft, the library and swimming pool drawn in and named with the aerodrome at its centre, two runways connected by a cross-run with the hardstandings to the northern end, the airfield looking like an esoteric symbol scraped into the landscape, a shape seen in a cave painting, a glyph from the old tongues, otherworldly, replete with lost meaning.

*

Letter #3

Come and get me lover boy come and get me I'm giving you two days to get here meet me where you said you would you promised don't dare not be there they got me Harper they got me.

I says nothings going to ruin me you remember I said that I'd enough ruining done on me to do a lifetime I was stupid I never seen them coming Upritchard says he wants to show me something downstairs he said it was a surprise that Cole had done for me it was a surprise you're worth nothing to them except what they can take from you bastards bastards bastards what they done to me they done to Ghost as well is this all my life to be held in rooms by men like them help me help me they made Cole cut sticks for them the poor little cur he didn't know what he was doing and they knew how far gone I was all I could think when they were doing it was baby baby

baby singing my baby songs in my head sweet songs from the films so the baby ears couldn't hear and the baby heart wouldn't be scared all it would hear is Mummy singing singing my little James or what her name would be if it's a girl!! Be there lover boy be there Sunday night I'll get out the fire escape after tea the usual place no kisses this time they dried up the kissing on me but not for ever.

Twenty-one

Morne
13th December 1944

Elspeth and Margaret giggling, walking home. You'd have thought they were drunk but they weren't. What was the film like, Lady in the Dark? Margaret asked. I don't know, Elspeth said, I hardly seen any of it, the face is kissed off me. Margaret said me too. They laughed the way girls do. We made a bet, Elspeth said, and wrote it down. A bet on what? Margaret said. On a kiss, Elspeth said, so tell us more about this Mr Strain, this man of yours. Margaret shook her head. Margaret the mystery women. She had always been like that. She wasn't a gossip and that suited Elspeth. She linked Margaret's arm, pulled her close. They could feel the warmth of each other, the girl-weight leaning in to each other, heads together, the steadying hold of each other's bodies, what it was to be linked home after a night's courting, your chin sore from his beard and other feelings all over your body, a kind of a far-off ache of measuring how far you could take him. They imagined themselves French girls coming home after an assignation. You have to watch yourself, Margaret said, they'll always try it on.

'Who?'

The two girls stopped. Elspeth looked back towards the

Avenue gates but they were far behind her, a square of moonlight, like a future dreamed of but fading. Both of them knowing that this was the worst thing that could ever happen to them.

'Who will always try it on?' Minister Davidson took them both by the elbow, separating them so that they were to either side of him, and like that he began to walk them towards the top of the Avenue.

'This is a pleasant stroll.' he said. 'Do you consider this a pleasant stroll, Miss Reilly?'

Margaret knew she didn't have to answer. Everything was laid bare. The girlish lies. The flimsy plots, hiding the way children hide when they think they can't be seen by adults. She thought she had never seen anything as white as Elspeth's face. There were so many stories about the Avenue and now it seemed that she was in one. They said that there was a red woman in the Avenue with long, strangling fingers. They said there were nuns, cowled figures from the past silently in procession through their lost cloisters. She wondered if there would be stories about them now, told in the schoolyard, two girls led away by the ghastly Minister, how a cold mist wreathed about them, their names whispered. Elspeth's face. Her eyes deep-sunk, mouth immobile, a masked player in this theatre of the night.

Twenty-two

Morne
28th November 2000

Black plastic bags had been piled at the door of the library. Mrs Orr helped Kay to carry them inside. Kay could smell must from her, the smell of the second-hand shop, forgotten drawers in back rooms, objects gathering dust in attics and the tops of wardrobes. Sometimes Kay would pick up a dress in the shop and hold it up to think of the girl who wore it, the tiny waists they had then twirling in front of the mirror ready to go out, picking out shoes, dainty patent pumps, trying out the dance steps on the bedroom floor. The lived day now come to this, a tarnished rack in a thrift shop, damp marks on the fabric, the hem frayed.

'These here chattels put the fear of God into me. They are the trumpery of the devil.'

Mrs Orr knew that something was at work in the town, shadow forces. From her bedroom above the shop she could hear waves booming against the harbour breakwaters, deep undersea sounds, ships' horns sounding out in the deep channels and being carried off in the north wind, the oceanic drift of things away from you. Last night she had sat at her dressing table looking out over the frozen rooftops of the town and had seen a single flare sent up over the lough, hanging in the air, lodestar to her fears. The flare had hung unextinguished in the night air for a long time and no one came until it sank towards the water and went out. She lay awake thinking about mariners cast adrift, being carried out to sea on frozen currents.

'It's only an exhibition,' Kay said, 'to get people to read more. About the war.' There were to be books on D-Day. On the war in the Atlantic. She had ordered texts on the Ardennes and the war in the air.

'It'll be the last time Lynch comes around the Post Office.'

'What do you mean it's the last time he'll be around?'

'You never heard,' Mrs Orr said. 'Lynch's gone missing feared drowned in the harbour.'

Kay heard music in the street. She went to the window. A group of Brethren at the corner of the Hollow. A wooden placard placed in front of them read 'The Wages of Sin Is Death'. The easterly blew ice particles from shop awnings and car roofs and the sleet blew into the faces of the faithful. The men wore overcoats and the woman wore anoraks and scarves tied around their heads. Their noses and lips were blue with cold. They wanted to be seen as huddled, windswept. They would raise their voices against the tempest.

Lorna among the other women, her hymnbook held before her. Upritchard stood at the front. His eyes were red-rimmed and he was unshaven. He looked consumed with knowledge. They were among the last days, given over to rapture.

Kay knelt on the floor and opened the bags. A box of '78 records in brown cardboard sleeves. She didn't recognise any of the names on the labels. A water-spotted Life magazine with George Patton on the cover. A tarnished 5th Airborne cap badge. A ration tin. A bale of camouflage netting. A paratrooper's boot with the sole torn off. Map holders, empty water canteens, belt webbing laid out on the library floor like battlefield detritus, testament of the unnamed.

Cole came to the library at lunchtime. Mrs Orr watching him from the thrift shop doorway. She had that wartime look. She wore belted dresses. Shoes with Cuban heels. She carried a patent handbag. He could see the look she gave him. Recognised him as a renegade from candid living.

Kay brought him down into the basement. More than history in the uniforms and catalogued militaria. There was a reaching out. Drawn in against her will.

'Lynch's not coming back,' Cole said. 'Word is he slipped on the ice and fell into the harbour basin somewhere around the container yard.'

'I just wanted an exhibition,' she said. She wanted civics, deep-seated values on display, the people of the town turning out for exhibitions, a holding together against adversity. Not this feeling that something was afoot.

She knelt at the box of records, separating the cardboard sleeves with her fingernails, lifting one out and allowing the weight of the black disc to carry it clear of the plain card sleeve.

The Blue Skirt Waltz.

She brought it to the phonograph, holding it by the edges, a black paten borne to ceremony. She put it on the turntable and started the mechanism. As she stepped back it clicked and whirred, the chrome arm moving onto the spinning black disc, the whole thing like a carnival chest of mysteries. Starting with accordions, it was the music of lost places. Polkas from the old country, danced at the edge of the forest as darkness fell.

'It's simple. A box step. You count the beats?' He shook his head. 'My dad taught me.'

She moved across the floor, stepping backwards, her hands high, her eyes fixed where a man's face might be if it were bent to hers. As though a partner assembled from the shadows led her in dance.

As she danced Cole was moving among the compiled documentation, at home with the smudged typefaces, the requisitions and ID documents. Kay put on another record. A South Sea sound, a lost hula in quickstep with brass coming in behind, Tommy Dorsey or Glenn Miller, shimmying girls in grass skirts, swaying under the palm trees, in the deep shade. Cole was turning uniform collars inside out, checking battledress pockets. Following the thread, putting it together. There was a forensics of the heart, sciences of the felt world. These objects hadn't come to Kay by accident.

'What are you doing?' He had made a small pile of documents and set down a tunic and battledress trousers, both turned inside out.

'Gabriel Hooper. Gabriel Hooper. Here's his service number. It's on this canteen and on the battledress jacket. GS 226854688.'

He went through the jacket pockets, Kay watching his hands, the way the jacket was rifled, the way he felt along the seams and lining and turned up the collar to look underneath it. Soft thieves' hands it looked like, searching out the hidden places. She remembered his hands on her in the Avenue. How men were there to take from you, the feeling of what was ransacked, left broken and empty.

He found a folded handbill in the breast pocket of the tunic. Before he could unfold it she reached out and took it from his hand.

'Give me that.' She opened it out. It was a cinema handbill. She was getting tired of these documents coming out of the past, elusive, coded. She was a librarian. There were systems, information catalogued and indexed. Rows of books numbered on the spine.

The Vogue Cinema
Lady in the Dark

Starring Ginger Rogers and Ray Milland
Friday 13th December 1944

'What's going on?'

'I'm here for a client.'

'The Vogue. It says the Vogue. The cinema you went to. The place you talked about.'

'I was a resident. In the home. The old hospital. Two older residents looked after me when I was there.'

'Reay.'

'And her boyfriend. Michael Harper.'

'He's your client.'

'Yes. In a way.'

'In a way means nothing.'

Kay thinking of the photograph she wasn't supposed to see. Reay and Harper on the edge of the water. The photograph, she thinks, is like something you would see in a magazine. Taken by a fashion photographer. The Kennedys or some other family knowing themselves favoured, gazing at the camera, splashing in the sea margins, sun-dazzled and unironic, knowing their own epic force, doom gathering at the edges of the frame.

'Harper,' he said and stopped.

Go on, she said to herself, there's a time to tell the truth and a time not to.

'He's dead.'

'Dead of what?'

Dead of provisional living in the lee of the slag heaps of Black Laws, Cole thought. Figures you see in the lost urban spaces, hoods pulled down, mayhem in their eyes, what's left of the thoughtful alone in the world, lost to bleak fated manhoods.

'I went back to my ma in Black Laws,' Cole said. 'Studied. Got a degree. I used to see Harper about the town. He wouldn't look at me, never mind talk.'

Cole meeting Harper outside on the slide bars, the disinterested look, sentiment an insult to memory, you're never going to speak her name, mention the hut by the edge of the sea, the girl dancing in the shallow water, all that was good in the world too fragile to be spoken of. Cole getting the law jobs nobody wanted, seeing Harper's name on court lists. There were squatted houses, adjourned appearances, bench warrants issued, minor epics, everyone knowing the score. Fighting the lost cause of himself.

'I got a letter saying they'd found a body in Morne. I went

looking for Harper but he'd died of septicaemia in the hospital. He was buried and I never heard.' Cole had looked for the grave but could not find it among the new graves and there was a grace in that he thought, that Harper might lie alone among the fallen. Cole found out where Harper had lived and went up there. Women pushing shopping trolleys through abandoned town precincts. Solemn children who looked as if they had taken vows of disappointment. The flat begrimed, cracked windows, flies in the kitchen. The place like a crime scene. You expected to see incident tape, blood spatter, an outflung arm on a bedroom floor.

The photographs were in a drawer in the bedroom. The Polaroids and the photograph of the two boys. Harper had hidden them under clothing. Love's a contraband you can't afford to be caught with, a border run in the dead of night, the pursuit not far behind. Cole put the photographs in his pocket. Because they'd met in a home, dressed in second-hand clothes, princelings of destitution shipped out together.

'Reay wrote to him. He never answered. He never came for us. It wouldn't have worked anyway.'

'I think we should have a look at this cinema.'

'Why?'

'Somebody wants us to.'

She read the address of the cinema. Sugar Island. The area between the back of the warehouses and the start of the aerodrome. There'd been Victorian teahouses up there, archive photographs of gardens with pergolas, ladies playing tennis in crinolines. Histories every town gathered to itself to say that it had not always been like this, the built areas crumbling, the population in decline, whole tracts unsafe after dark. There had been pre-war eras with men and women promenading on the front, times of civility, men in white playing sport, women watching from wooden pavilions.

Sugar Island's tennis courts and teahouses had been razed after the war and replaced by playing fields no longer used. There was broken glass on the pitches, the goalposts rotten and fallen down. Teenagers lit fires of driftwood on the seaward side of the pitches, signal fires, though they did not know who they signalled to, and no one came.

*

The wind is gathering in the deep mountain valleys above the lough, in the high meadows, the lone plateaux. Vast air movements in the scree slopes and unsheltered barrens. It'll build up there, the air masses meeting, columns of warm air a hundred fathoms high turning against each other. A thaw building.

*

Lily awake. The night still. Hear curlew on the lough. Shiftings in the icy sea grasses and reeds of the bents. Tiny, starved sounds. She know what moves in the dark and what tracings of themselves they leave and she named the imprints on the snow crust for what they were, the crow and the gull, fox with his brush. Know mouse froze in burrow. Die abed him the mouse. The scratched-at frost. The carrion hunters making count of that night's dead, making toll of them. Know what things of dark walk the shoreline.

She heard a car stop outside the chalet. The road was still with cold. Frozen mist on the machair channels and the stumps of old trees protruding above the mist gave the shore the look of a graveyard from a gas-lit drama, the dead risen from their graves to walk abroad, a staged feel to the night.

Lily wondered which figure of the past came calling at such an hour. She bundled up her work and put it into the Hope chest. There were footsteps on the concrete path. Lily looked through the side window of the porch and saw a dark shape, a small black-gloved hand, widowed, tapping on the door.

'Who you?' Lily said. 'Go way.'

'It's me, Lily. Rebecca.'

'Use your right name.'

'Please, Lily.' The Matron heard Lily tugging at the door. The door bolted shut, the bolts seized to their tangs with frost. Lily had to work them from their housing.

'I thought you weren't going to let me in,' the Matron said. Lily looked down at the bolts, flakes of old paint on the hall-way tiles. 'Can I step in? It's cold.'

'You look like die,' Lily said.

'I feel close to it.'

'Magistrate gone.'

'Are you not going to offer me your sympathy?'

'No.'

'I thought that. He was a bad man who did bad things.'

'Say you now.'

'I said it before too.'

'No good then. No good now.'

'That is gone now, Lily.'

'Use right name.'

'Margaret.'

'And your name Elspeth.'

Their names had been carried away, blown like rain across the marshland. Lily minded looking out of the window at night watching lights moving across the back of the dunes, men from the city after hares. She had forgotten them and when Kay told her again what the men were doing she thought of the hares, their unnamed selves alone in the moonlight.

The Matron walked carefully. Her gauntness moved with her like a shadow, her body all hollows, absences. She stood in the doorway like an edifice with dark history attached to it. A place you wouldn't go after nightfall.

'Near done.'

'Yes. Near done, Margaret.'

'They take away our names.'

'They took more than our names.'

'What for?'

'For a kiss. A kiss in the dark.'

'A kiss.'

'You remember the night they stole our names?'

'Remember me.' Lily's eyes looked yellow in the dark.

Kingdom Hall
16th December 1944

As you were named so be ye renamed

It was to be a naming ceremony. The Reverend Davidson stood at his preacher's table. Elspeth and Margaret sat at the rear of Kingdom Hall, apart from the congregation and from each other. Witness was given as to Elspeth's promiscuity. Witness was given as to Margaret's deceit in support of Elspeth's sinning with the black man. When their names were spoken the girls were to stand.

The cinema owner McKee said that he saw Elspeth go into the back row of the cinema although Margaret knew that it was too dark for him to see anything of the kind. Margaret knew McKee liked to go up the back entry of Crutchley's bar and there drink miniature whiskeys in the back room. It was said that when the cinema audience went home other men joined McKee in the cinema to watch films of a depraved nature. His was a gaze that lingered over women's stockinged legs. He had loose lips, red like ripe cherries.

The Minister asked McKee if he could see who Elspeth kept company with. McKee said it was a soldier. When the Minister asked what kind of a soldier it was clear what he meant.

The congregation sat in silence. The women's long hair tied back from their foreheads with a scarf, plain-looking, shriven. The men wore black suits. The elders sat in a semi-circle to one side. Elspeth stood before them, her head down and her hands clasped in front of her like an illustration of Penance from the First Bible Reader.

They knew who she was. Succubus. Hollow-cheeked. Ravening.

McKee said that it was a darkie soldier. The congregation sat without moving. They felt that they had found themselves within the text of a reading, one of the apocalyptic books where demons burst forth and took upon themselves the pleasing shapes of womanhood. They felt themselves under the jaded gaze of harlots.

'One of the children of Ham who was accursed by his own father Noah, who was seen in his nakedness?' the Minister said.

'One of the children of Ham,' McKee said, 'that's what he was, Reverend.' Margaret knew that the children of Ham were dark of skin.

Margaret was told to stand and approach the table. She looked at the path between seats that led to the semi-circle of elders, the long shaming walk on the wax-polished board. Elspeth said they kept it that way so that the elders could see up their skirts.

Each footfall sounded like the loudest thing in the world. She glanced up as she passed the last row of seats and saw Wesley Upritchard sat beside his friends Lynch and Corry. Wesley shaped the word *Hore* with his lips, wiping his mouth afterwards.

She stood before the elders but she could not lift her head. She could see one of Elspeth's black Sunday shoes in the corner of her eye. She knew that Elspeth hated them, the way they wouldn't take a shine, the boxy shape, it was like putting your feet into two coffins she said.

Davidson was the patient shepherd. Margaret was a member of the flock who had wandered. Margaret had watched the wartime films, the plucky girl-spies caught and tortured, refusing to give up names, the flash of defiance in the face of the firing squad. She had wanted to be like that but the Minister would not let her. She felt him draw her into a grave parable of sin and redemption. She had found herself led by Elspeth off the path of righteousness. She had not known what man did unto woman in the back seats of the cinema save that they sinned. Elspeth had led her to it.

Elspeth was told to stand in her turn. Davidson spoke without looking at her. The creature before him was pathetic. She would be sent from the congregation as would a soiled rag or a broken instrument. Blood was not greater than shame. Among the Fallen there must be one who is Saved. She would be Shunned. One by one the Brethren stood and confirmed the Shunning. Margaret kept her head down. Elspeth's foot unmoving at the edge of her sightline, the coffin shoe. She could feel the words of renouncing coming off her tongue, the damning of her friend.

'Margaret shall take as her new name Lily, for she is as the lily of the valley, shining and reborn.'

The Minister turned to his daughter. Elspeth had not lifted her head.

'You were given the name Elspeth, meaning pledged to God, when you were born. You have broken that pledge by your actions. Your name from this night out is Rebecca.'

'Why Rebecca, father? Why do you name me thus?' The girl's voice was quiet.

'For you know to whom Rebecca was betrothed.'

After the service Margaret waited behind with her parents. When the congregation was gone Davidson took them into the Minister's room. He took the statement she had made in relation to the accusation against Gabriel Hooper. He added another paragraph. She put her signature to it.

*

Cole lay awake in the caravan. Wind channelled down the lough from the mountains, the ice starting to melt. Formerly the tide had carried industrial effluents sluiced from the mills and dyeworks at the headwaters to the mouth of the lough. The beach covered in stagnant weed to the high-tide mark. And the wind had carried away the odours of the town, the mill-reek and lint-stink, and brought instead the sounds of the town, a death ballad chanted in the breeze. He got up and sat at the banquette until dawn. He heard Kay stir. She sat up and wrapped her dressing gown around her, put her feet into slippers. Small chaste gestures. He thought of her during the night. She wanted him to murmur words in her ear. Fuck. Cunt. Her face buried in the pillow. She sat down beside him at the banquette. There were dark shadows under her eyes. She looked haggard, guilt-ridden. As though the filthy words having once been said could not be withdrawn, the whispered depravities.

Sometime during the night she had risen and removed her make-up. The self in the mirror had to be scrubbed, earnest. He leaned towards her and touched her thigh and felt her withdraw. This was not her, the painted jade of night's desire. Her face was scrubbed now. This is who I am. Plain of heart.

He looked out, the beach scoured by the tide, dark weed and empty tins of anti-foulant. On the blockhouse island cormorants held their wings outstretched.

'It's to hide their shame.'

'Shame?'

'They say the cormorants carry messages to the under-world. They hold their wings like that to conceal their heads, to hide their shame.'

'They might be needed in this town.'

'They might be.'

On the blockhouse island, the cormorants crouched in rows, their black ragged wings banners to the lost armies of the dawn.

Twenty-three

Shepton Mallet
30th January 1945

Davis watched Hooper's cell window. He told the others about the agonies of mind the Negro must be going through. 'His guilt like a red-hot needle, men, piercing his very soul.' The others had stopped listening to Davis but they lay in their bunks thinking about Hooper. How his nights would be. Sleepless, pacing.

Hooper joined the prison library. The chaplain offered him religious tracts and spoke of the path to salvation but Hooper asked for books such as the Illustrated History of Flying and The Story of the Wright Brothers. If he had time, he told the chaplain, he would build a replica of their plane, the crafted, spindly thing borne aloft on prairie breezes. He would use balsa woods and fine epoxy resins, so light that when it left the ground it would never touch earth again. He would fly over those destroyed cities of the Rhineland he had seen in the Bomb Loft but they would not be ruined, they would be shining and exalted and would raise themselves up before him.

The morning of the verdict he rose and put on his dress uniform and waited for the MPs to fetch him. Phair had not been to see him in the period since the last hearing and he took that as a sign that things would not go well. Hooper marched across the front yard between two MPs. Halfway across the yard he dragged his heel on the cobbles and sparks arced out behind his foot. He could feel the following MPs' eyes on him.

Hooper was escorted into the court martial room and stood to attention. The Adjutant General and his two judges sat at their table. Phair did not look around when he came in. Dupont leaned back, one arm thrown over the back of the chair. There was a half-smile on his face, a distance in his eyes. He looked like a man remembering the heat of a southern noon, a corpse gibbeted from a bough, a rope creaking.

The MPs withdrew. Hooper stood on his own. He looked over at the evidence table to see if Elspeth's clothing was still there but it had been removed. The Judge Advocate asked him if he had anything to say.

'What'll happen to them, Sir?' Hooper said.

'What will happen to what, Private?'

'Elspeth's clothes. What will happen to them?'

'They'll be sent back to her.' Phair looked at him, wondering if Hooper wished to hang himself twice over by referring to the victim's underclothing.

'Evidence will be returned on conclusion of the proceedings.'

'Don't open your mouth again,' Phair said, 'for Christ's sakes man, you're in deep enough as it is.'

Hooper cared that Elspeth was always in the room when they were there, scantily clad, vulnerable. That the garments were hers, close-fitted to her body, carrying the heat of it, the beloved form. The Adjutant General began to read.

'That on the thirteenth of December at the place know as the Avenue in the town of Morne, you did feloniously assault and carry out an act of rape against the person of Elspeth Davidson . . .

'That this court finds the accused Gabriel Hooper guilty of this charge . . .

'That in the absence of extenuating circumstance and in accordance with the policy of the United States Government in matters involving outrage against citizens of allied countries, this court martial can permit itself only one judgement . . .

'That the guilty party Private Gabriel Hooper, of the sixth district Atlanta Georgia, have the lawful sanction of execution awarded to him, said sanction to be carried out within twenty-four hours of the delivery of this judgement and may God have mercy on his soul.'

'I won my bet,' Hooper said.

'The convicted man will be quiet.'

'I only remembered, Sir. I won my bet in the Vogue. The Walking Liberty. Else she would have it. Elspeth. We wrote the bet on the seat in the Vogue. We carved it in the wood with the edge of the silver half-dollar, date and all. It's proof. It's proof you're all wrong.'

The MPs moved to either side of Hooper. They had heard it before on sentencing, the disordered mutterings, the invoking of higher authority. Men looked around wildly as if they might escape. They collapsed on the floor, they looked uncomprehendingly at their counsel. What men said in the shadow of the gallows. What men did. They took Hooper by the elbows and turned him towards the door. Phair ran his hands through his hair wearily. Dupont glanced at him as though to ask on what grounds he imagined himself entitled to theatrical gesturing.

The Death Cell, Shepton Mallet
Dawn, 31st January 1945

If Hooper turned he would see Lindbergh towering darkly over him, his eyes glinting in the shadow of his brows like faraway constellations. He would speak with a drawl. He would take Hooper around the plane, show him the landing gear, show him the wings, a hand placed on his shoulders explaining how the flaps worked for lift and together they would catch the sweet winds aloft.

The work detail had passed Phair in the yard the previous night. There was mud on their boots. They had used picks to open the frozen ground for Hooper's grave. A galvanised barrel of quicklime had been placed in the execution yard. The burial detail gloved and masked to sprinkle the corrosive dust into the blackness of the grave. They wore hoods to cover their heads and necks, and Phair glimpsed them through the half-open gates of the burial yard as he passed on the way to his office. The men were talking as they worked and one laughed and another turned to stare at him through the gate in silence. The hoods they had made themselves from scrap material in a variety of colours and Phair remembered his New Orleans childhood and pierrots and conjurors in the street below his window.

When he entered his office Dupont was sitting on the edge of his desk. The skin around his eyes creased in what might pass for a smile. As though some irony of the Deep South came to him as he looked at Phair. Words that were drawled homespun yarns told as the evening deepened and night crept from the edge of the world.

'Can I help you?' Phair said.

'Not so much.'

'You'll excuse me. I'm busy.'

'You'll be filing the paperwork on the boy they hanged this morning.'

'I'm almost done.'

'The paperwork is incomplete. If I were you I'd leave it that way.'

'I don't know what you're talking about.'

'This is what I'm talking about.' Dupont placed an opened envelope on the desk.

'What is it?'

'Look.'

To the Court Martial of Gabriel Hooper
10th January 1945

My name is Elspeth Davidson. I am daughter and only child to the Reverend Davidson of the Elected Brethren in the County Ward of Morne. I am sixteen years of age. I am housekeeper to my father since my mother has gone before us in the Lord and a member of the Ladies' Committee of the Brethren committed to God's work in the town. In the course of my duties I made the acquaintance of an American soldier by the name of Gabriel Hooper who is now in court

237

accused in front of you as I believe. I am writing to say that my father
has given you a document which contains untruths and says shameful
things about Gabriel Hooper. I do not know why he has done this
but he says I must respect his choice as he is Elected and that is true.
But I know that I cannot see a man blamed in the wrong and subject
to your wrath and judgement. I have kept accounts of all encounters
and can testify, you only have to ask. My father says that I am a viper
and that it would have been better if he had not nurtured me under
his roof and had instead put me aside, and has me betrothed to a
boy who helped him in his false accusation. I may answer for my sins
before the 'dread seat' but I cannot be silent under happenings such as
these where a man might lose all for want of true testimony.
   Yours respectfully,
   Elspeth Davidson

'When did this come?'

'I just saw it.'

'It's postmarked the tenth.'

'Things get lost in wartime.'

'He wouldn't have been hanged.'

'He was hanged the minute he put his hands on her.'

Phair held the letter up to the light. Written in blue ink. A
looping hand. Watermarked Basildon Bond.

'Her address is on it. Send it back. Say it came too late.
Matter of fact it was too late before she sent it.'

Twenty-four

Morne
29th November 2000

It's Saturday night. The weather is breaking, the thaw is on and they're coming into town. Girls in heels and stockings, the moment given a 1950s look, beehives and falsies. Brassy and tottering with Smirnoff naggins in their handbags. Security in evening dress and black tie, hair slicked back so you're thinking Ronnie and Reggie. There's a police dive crew from out of town at the harbour looking for Lynch's body. The night gathering in layers. Somebody's going to get their smile widened with a razor. Somebody's going to end up as roadfill.

At the swimming pool you could see distant ships riding beyond the bar, their masthead lights against the darkness of the channel reaching up to the constellations, as though to mend with light the broken parts of the world. The mountains on the far side of the lough stood clear and outlined against the sky. The water cold with snowmelt.

Once the earth and sky were put apart there would be no joining them again. Kay pushed off from the wall and swam in a crawl, lengths that seemed to be a kind of dreaming, the black seawater folding on itself in front of her and returning to itself behind her, Kay breathing on the uproll.

She stopped at the far end of the pool and lifted herself on her arms onto the pool edging. Her body weight on her bare arms and shoulders, night's gymnast pauses on the rings. Beads of seawater chill on her flesh. Harbour light. The swimsuit's damp material puckered at her thighs.

She went into the roofless changing rooms and started to undress, taking the straps from her shoulders and lowering the swimsuit to her waist. She reached out for her clothes.

She knew by now that shadows detached themselves, that they did not stay where they belonged. This one was Wesley Upritchard, adrift from the wall, but it could have been others. Kay could put names to them all. Upritchard moved between Kay and her clothes. She stood in front of him, the swimsuit folded at her waist. She wished there was an old-fashioned god she could pray to, a kindly god of cracked statues on dusty windowsills.

'Did Corry say anything?' Upritchard said.

'What?'

'Did he say anything? Dying words? A final statement?'

'No.'

'You crossed the river. You swam to the back of Corry's house.'

'I'm a swimmer. The man who called himself my father gave me that. Among other things.'

'Corry gave you your mother's letters?'

'They were mine.'

'Where's Lynch?' He followed her eyes to the Brighter Morn, the half-sunk wreck canted against the lido wall.

'It took me a long time, but I can see your mother in you. In your eyes.'

'Is that so?'

'It is. I can see the tramp in you. I can see the whore.'

'Don't call her that.'

'The way of things. The daughter follows the mother. Black cat, black kitten.'

Kay held her bra in her right hand, the indented under-thing, the hard nylon carapace like a found part of the ocean, an emptied-out sea casing. The harbour water still beyond the pool wall, waveless, the silence of last things.

'You gave me away. To Kenny.'

'The Matron did that. Her and Dr Eugene.'

She recalled Kenny, the man who called himself her father. He had a tattoo on his arm. When she was small she thought it was a flower but now she knew it for a submariner's tattoo, twin screws, and she wished Kenny fathoms deep beneath the waves, in the godless depths.

'I've been keeping an eye on you,' he said. The camera pointed at her caravan, Upritchard staring at the bedroom window, imagining the interior, the fold-down bed, the mattress thin and worn out. He imagines Kay's assignations over the years, a little bit seedy, a little bit melancholy. The marks of bra straps on her skin. The marks of elastic on her hips. Upritchard watching Cole arriving at the caravan and his leaving, closing the aluminium door behind him, lean-ing back against it and running his hand through his hair. Upritchard imagines the complex needs, the sating, the feel of old acrylic fabrics on her skin, the caravan smell. He won-ders who has been there in the caravan before Cole, what small-town lusts have been given full rein, the caravan rock-ing on the hissing sand.

Upritchard like an embalmed thing, his skin yellow and

ghastly in the carbide light from the harbour. Kay standing before him, eyes cast down, a roadside madonna.

'I have to get dressed.'

'It makes no difference to me.'

'Where are we going?'

'You'll see.'

Cole drove out to the Limekiln road. The stones of the limekiln tumbled to the foreshore, the fire of the kiln gone out and never relit. He stepped over the low ditch and started to make his way along the estuary. The water in the channel seemed to rustle. He looked down and saw that it was full of elvers, the juvenile eels driven to migrate by the moon phase. The thaw under way. The east wind blew cloud against the sides of the mountain. A wildness that he did not understand was all about him. He saw a figure dressed in white out by the big rock at the channel opening. He made his way along the mud banks.

When he got there he saw that it wasn't a rock. It was an aero engine from a crashed plane, the metal fused with rust, the airframe long gone. The blades had shattered but the boss of the propeller was intact. Lily was holding on to one of the bent cooling fins. She was looking west to the gap in the mountains. She was wearing the wedding dress from her Hope chest. The wind plucked at it in a way that reminded him of hurt wildfowl, the injured fluttering. The sleeves were stained and the thread holding the decorative beading on the hem and bodice had disintegrated so that the wind stripped the beads from the cloth and the sequins carried away in the wind made a long white slipstream behind her.

They were at the apex of the flightpath to the main runway.

Cole could feel the mud liquefy under his feet and hear the tidal surge pushing over the bar.

'Kay said you were making a shroud.'

'No shroud,' Lily said. 'Wedding dress.'

Cole took her arm to lead her back to land but she stopped him and pointed west and for a moment he thought he could see the memory that had brought Lily there.

'I lost me,' Lily said. On the way back she moved her head slowly from side to side as if the nightfall she had known all her life had been replaced with another that was unfamiliar. It wouldn't do the things you wanted of the darkness. The way you expected it to behave.

Cole took her up to the bedroom, wrapping her in blankets and waiting until she fell asleep. When he came downstairs the wind had blown the back door open and had entered the room, stripping Lily's writings from the walls. The air was filled with blown paper, ghostly notes. Cole closed the door and started to pick up the notes. The door strained against its hinges as though something sought entry. Among the notes he found a letter.

Pirnmill Airbase
1st February 1945

Dear Miss Reilly,
It is with deep regret that I wish to inform you of the loss of Flight Officer Daniel Strain. Flight Officer Strain's aircraft was lost with all crew missing presumed dead during a flight operation in the Ruhr valley on 20th December 1944. Flight Officer Strain spoke often of you and of your marriage plans. His loss is felt deeply here. Our air

crews have taken quite a pounding and this is the seventeenth aircraft we have lost.

Yours faithfully,
Group Captain John Frost

*

Cole thought of the hawk she had hung on the outhouse door, the hunt, the silence of things taken in the air.

Lily called from upstairs. She was sitting up in bed. There was some urgent telling she couldn't get to. Cole showed her the letter. Oscar Tango Charlie, Lily said. He had no idea if it was the memory she had been seeking. In any case her airman had been gone too long. If he came back now he would not be the same. He would have the cold light of distant stars in his eyes, far constellations.

In the war years her mother had said not to even look on the soldiers. There were stories of girls taken into fields. But Lily would sit on the landing windowsill and watch for them, driving under blackout with their headlights taped up. The pilots in the back with sheepskin flying jackets, faces lit as they drew on a cigarette. Their passing left exhaust fumes and the smell of black tobacco in the air.

You could see the red flare of the plane exhausts as they came in from the mission, frail fire in the night. Lily waited through the years. She walked the Limekiln road looking at the sky for signs, the heavy-engine sound between the mountains, the pitch and yaw of the wings, the landing lights coming on, guiding them home over the sand flats and channels.

Lily spoke into the night. Lily said it was cold the year she was born. Frost to the tideline. The stunted birches at the back of the chalets turned black. Spirit animals emerged from the frozen landscape and addressed her. She talked about the hares on the dunes. How strangers lamped and then trapped them and you could hear their squeals coming across the water.

Cole sat by her bed, Lily getting agitated. Terror in her eyes. Some tale of figures standing around in the dark that she couldn't get to. Cole made tea and held the cup to her mouth.

'Told me her,' Lily said.

'You told somebody something?' Cole said.

'What they done.'

'Who?'

'See them put girl in the sandpit.'

'Reay?'

'Was that girl's name?'

'Yes.'

'Me stand outside at night. Watch the sky. Watch for his plane. Seen them with her.'

'Corry, Lynch and Upritchard.'

'Them's the ones.'

'Who did you tell, Lily?' Lily giving him a sly look.

'Lily not tell.'

'Whisper it.'

'Lily not tell tale.'

'Whisper it in my ear.' He leaned forward. He could feel her breath against his face. Lily's breath smelt estuarine, of brines and saltmarsh, old wracks heaped on a distant shoreline.

Outside the wind had blown the sparrowhawk from the outhouse wall and scattered what remained of it. Cole took up the skull and picked off the bristles and pin feathers between the eyes and beak. The yellow discs of the eyes had hardened and turned translucent. There was dark meat attached to the underside of the head and dried sinew where the spinal cord had attached, but the skull cavity was empty as though the cased matter behind the eyes had always been air, as though emptiness was all there had ever been of it.

*

The morgue in the basement. Upritchard led Kay down a stairwell. She feels herself part of the workhouse complex. She can feel herself deep in the ground. She can feel its fastness all around her, the earthhold.

Steel-framed beds were stacked head-high against the walls. Kay thought of nurses in old-fashioned starched uniforms. Nuns in habits and wimples, bringers of succour. You thought of them enclosed and mendicant, supplication murmured through convent grilles. Not these death-haunted environs.

Upritchard opened the morgue door. Chipped tiling to waist level. Above that the walls were distempered, the paint peeling and flaked, the ground-damp seeping upwards. There was rubber matting on the floor worn through to the concrete in places. Theatre lights from long ago were switched on over the autopsy bench. The fittings were stiff and tarnished and Upritchard adjusted the nearest so that its brass pivot squealed.

Upritchard slid the cadaver drawer. The body was chilled but Kay could smell the ground from which it had been taken. The stench of the opened pit.

246

'I don't want to look. Shut it. Please.'

She did not look again at what lay in the drawer. The figure seemed wizened and hag-like, come to her from some dream of corruption and she wished not to know her.

Upritchard crossed the room to the stainless steel shelving units. There were jars and kidney dishes on the shelves. You thought of them filled with viscera, the organs stored for journey as they might be for a pharaoh or his queen.

'Her clothes.' He threw an evidence bag on the floor.

'Please. Why are you doing this?'

He used scissors to cut the cable tie on the evidence bag. He laid the clothing on the sterile surface, the odour of ground toxins rising from the fabrics. The material starting to stiffen. He placed the clothes as she would have worn them, stained beyond recognition and shrunken by long immersion to a child's proportions.

'A child's clothes,' Kay said, 'they look like a child's clothes.'

'The size on the label. It's a ten. Tights. Shoes size six. No child was wearing this outfit.'

'Not her.'

'Jeans. Some kind of sweater.' The arm of the sweater crooked in a cold and godless beckoning. The material of the brassiere twisted and sodden. Pit dirt ingrained in its decorative panelling.

'There's a blouse as well.'

Grave artefacts. The clothing was shrunken with age, the garments of some long-dead child king.

'Cheesecloth.'

'It's her, isn't it? Lily saw you put her in the ground. She told me.'

Cheesecloth. Reay. Her back against the sun-warmed planks.
If she had a chance she said she'd live there for ever.

'Who put the photo through my door?'

'It was in his briefcase.'

'I am a man who lives alone. It scared me.'

'No more scaring than you deserve.' Dr Eugene stood in the doorway. He was wearing a black overcoat over pyjamas. His feet were bare and blue with cold, gashed on the sole and instep. He was unshaven. His hair stood out from his head. Kay thought of a fabled man-beast from an old book of hours, a folkloric terror, something that came down from the stark mountainside at the coming of night to take what was his.

Twenty-five

Morne
29th November 2000

The front door lay open and the north-west wind had blown snow through it onto the wood of the hallway, all across the fine herringbone. A wind vortex spinning in the porch had carried the snow into the drawing room where it still lay powdery, unmelted on the worn silk rug in front of the fireplace and on the hem of the Matron's dress. She sat unmoving in front of a cold grate, blind to all but regret. The temperature outside was still below zero but it was not more chill than memory.

There was a bottle of Black & White whisky on the table and a soda syphon beside it. She liked using the syphon, the lab flask feel to it, the valve hiss. Sent to London by her father in the post-war years. She'd started work in the hospital lab. Bunsen burners and their gas hoses. The rubbery coils hanging in cupboards, the douches and enemas. The cultures seething in the petri dishes. She had seen the girls. *Looking a nice time, soldier.*

Brought in ruptured. The enemas. The coat hangers. Putting corrosives into themselves, drinking gin. They couldn't be told to stay away from the soldiers. What the uniform did to a girl. The moment she set eyes on Dr Eugene she knew what he was. He had the odour of the backstreet clinic about him, and the black bag he carried, she knew what instruments it would contain.

Snow flurries drifted through the door, spun by the indraught into a dainty processional across the polished floor that sounded to her like skirts brushing the wood. Phantoms. Cole came in with them. She did not look up at him.

'Reay.'

'Reay died of a pulmonary embolism as she was giving birth. I worked on her with Eugene. It was a wild night. I thought the windows would come in around us.'

Giving birth in the dentist's chair. The Matron hearing her cry out in the night. Reay's back raised with welts from the sally rods. The child wrapped in towels, swaddled. The winds that blow on high the gaunt building and its paupers' graves, the pine trees tossed in the gale. Winds from the north-west that night, the people of the town looking to sea for the masthead lights of trawlers offshore, unable to approach the bar, the Haulbowline light's glass shattered by a thirty-metre wave. The Matron gathered the child to herself and held it.

'The three of them took her to the sandpit. The Brethren, they called themselves.'

'You didn't let them take the baby.'

'They thought me unclean because I'd held hands with a black man. The law of leprosy. To teach when it is unclean and when it is clean. Leviticus chapter thirty-four. They shunned me. And then they had a wake for me. I held a baby out of wedlock in my unclean hands. They had no use for her.'

'Eugene took her.'

'He gave her to someone he had worked on ships with. The man and his wife had no children. He thought he could trust him but he could not. Kay is not who you think she is.'

'She told me about her childhood. It sounded happy. He took her swimming. He picked her up after concerts.'

She had said her bedroom windowsills were lined with teenage mementos, ticket stubs, band memorabilia. Friendships kept up, birthdays observed. The world kept at bay with the hard-earned and durable.

'It's not true. She was abused by them. They were people of the gutter. When social services came for her she was living in squalor. She was removed and placed in care.'

'He taught her to swim.'

'She learned to swim in care. They brought her to the pool every day. They thought it was therapeutic.'

'She collected things. Bits and pieces.'

'I know. I visited her. She stole things and hid them. The staff took them off her and gave them to me.'

A half-filled dance card. The skirt of a Chanel suit. Handbags. The scuffed and the lipstick-stained. A man's dress suit jacket with the tailor's mark on it.

Reay had kept things too, Cole remembered. Newspaper cuttings. Stories of fortitude, people who overcame terrible odds, who rose above things. Mothers of abducted children, lovers reunited after years apart. Yellowed clippings fell out of books. Astrology charts. Advice for the lovelorn.

'She's a librarian.'

'She worked in the hospital library when she was in care. They threw her out when she turned eighteen. I found her living in that old caravan, hardly able to feed herself. I brought her back to work here. The library belongs to the Brethren.'

'Corry knew?'

'Everyone knew.'

'You used her to get back at them.'

'After I was shunned I asked my father if I had put my eternal soul at hazard.'

'What did he say?'

'He said that to put your soul at hazard you have to possess one. Do you?'

'Why do you ask that?'

'Reay talked the whole time. She was asking for Harper. She said he never answered her letters. Harper never came back for her. Does a ghost have a soul?'

'I don't know.'

The Matron was standing. Cole could feel her cold breath on his cheek. 'Because if a ghost has a soul then you have lost yours, haven't you?'

'What do you mean?'

'You know very well what I mean. Reay told me she gave you her letters to Harper to post. "I gave them to Ghost," she said. "You can trust Ghost."'

'Did she say that?'

'You didn't post them.'

'They had each other. I had no one. If Harper took her away there would be no one.'

'She said they planned to come back for you.'

'Everyone says things like that, and no one comes back.'

Upritchard knew that Eugene was still in the building. The doctor had followed him from the basement, Upritchard moving through the service corridors and back stairs, through the ducting and broken floorboards, the copper wiring and pipework long since ripped out. Upritchard finding himself on the top floor, on the dormitory corridor, the dental surgery at the end of the corridor, the wind blowing the way it had done the night that Reay had died, the corridor planking and roof beams creaking, the windows loose in their frames. He had to pass the surgery where Reay had given birth to reach the fire escape and he did not look into the room. It resembled a resurrectionist's den of hasps and saws and bone files, the anatomy laid bare, and he had seen the floor underfoot awash with blood and had no desire to awaken the memory. Outside the wind pressed him back against the wall and the fire escape creaked and groaned. He remembered the Negro and that he had been hanged and wondered if he had gone to his death capped in black or bare-headed.

Upritchard looked down from the swaying and clanking fire escape. There was a car at the front of the building. The bare branches of a tree flail wildly in the top right corner. The car is a dark-coloured saloon. Kay's car. She walks from the hospital building to it. She looks like a figure from a newsreel, an old-time bootlegger. He feels like he's watching mono-chrome footage, the colours washed-out, security lighting on the front of the morgue, giving the scene a Cold War menace. A late-night border exchange. A double-cross on the cards.

The town laid out beneath him, a map of betrayal, the

night gathering, the empty warehouses reflected back in slub colours from the river, Upritchard thinking that if he looked he'd see the town's dead, their drowned faces, looking back at him from the water. He can see the cartographies of his ruin. The Matron and Lily mapping the town, downfalls plotted, gathering the evidence of the years in stolen letters, forbidden garments, planting them or giving them to Kay, artful as her mother.

He thinks he hears Eugene in the corridor, approaching the door behind him. The distant mountains lost to him now. The darkness of the fallen. The chapels. Lovers cast adrift from the tin-walled dance halls to walk the lanes for ever. Eels in the culverts. The winter feeding grounds. Iced-over shallows. The marram grass. White bones in the machair. The bidden shadows of the dead rise up and walk the lost pathways.

Ocean Sands Caravan Park
30th November 2000

Cole knowing he had been looking for sure ground in the wrong place. There were imprints on the concrete where the wheels of Kay's caravan had been, shore plants growing in the sand and shingle that had been driven across the runway and caught in the undercarriage of the caravan. Rust stains on the concrete where salt water had corroded the chassis. The milk crate that had been used as a step had been upturned with a stone placed in it to stop it blowing away, the hose of the water connection coiled and tied with cord, the world as orderly as you could make it, Kay making provision against things falling apart.

There was paper blowing across the concrete barrens of the aerodrome on the sea side of the caravan park. Damp, crumpled sheets. Reports, statements, letters. What she'd taken from Corry. What she'd been given by the Matron. Cole picked one up and flattened it out on the bonnet of the car. Above the lough a skein of geese crossed from east to west, the last of them, the migration routes empty until the autumn. On the blockhouse island the cormorants. The paper was old, disintegrating. The blue ink had run, carrying the words deep into the fabric of the paper, into the fibres of it, watermarked with hurt. Reay's last letter. He got into his car and drove towards Sugar Island.

The Vogue Cinema

The cinema stands alone on the Parade. Through the grimed glass panels in the front door you can see posters framed on the interior walls, stars of post-war cinema in pastels and ghosts of muted longing in the empty foyer. The liturgies of ruin.

Cole leaned against the door. The wood around the lock hasp had rotted and it gave way. They went in and he wedged the door behind them and the wind beat upon it like phantoms who sought entry but were forever pledged to the night. Cole moved slowly. He was in the presence of memory, his younger self and the selves of many, audience after audience, the shuffling others. They would not be hurried. He lit a match and crossed the dank foyer carpet to the fuse cupboard.

He pulled the trip switch on the Bakelite main fuse. A few bulbs came on, dusty and flickering. Mementos. Kay stood with one hand on the partition between screen and stalls and the other on her hip, acting it, wartime pin-up, marcelled and wholesome.

She came back and put her hand in his. He was wary of memory, the tricks of it, what sleight of hand awaited him in the dark. In the velvet balcony seats, dust motes in the projector beam.

They stood in the stalls looking towards the screen. The space demanded silence, stories told in the dark, the whispering reels. The filed-through generations had left something of themselves behind in the high-ceilinged space, the heart's affinities.

They climbed the steps into the balcony towards the double seats against the back wall, under the projector. The weighted velvet seat folded down. The armrests awkward. These were the spaces where the rules were set. For the breathless pause, the small, chaste touches. Each couple bent to their own custom and observance. The shiftings and touchings spreading out to the rest of the auditorium, the felt offering, the erotic force.

Kay put her head against the headrest. Desire. Cole knowing that he was expected to be clumsy, that she would murmur, take his hand from her breasts, that everything would be about what was withheld, just out of reach.

'You see this?' She took a lighter from her bag and leaned forward, holding the light to the varnished wooden casing of the seat in front.

'Look.' He saw the varnish was scraped in places. She held

the flame closer. Names incised in the laminate. Jake, Flatbush Avenue Brooklyn, 20th Jan 1944. There were others. E. Boone, Chicago, July 1944. He felt a sense of discovery, of old things unearthed. Cave tracings. The varnish flaked on the curve of a letter where the milled edge of the coin had dragged at it. 5th Airborne. Cole thinking of the soldiers crouched in the dark, etching their names, suddenly serious, giving thought to the task. Cromie. Bell. Michaels. Ezekiel. Her face beside him, underlit by the flame.

'Here,' she said, 'some of them had girls with them.' Ben and Edith. Frank and Molly. A heart drawn beside a girl's name. Newell, McGlade, Heyman.

You could imagine the names chanted, sung out, talisman against the gathering dark. Kay's face shadowed, serious.

She touched one of the names, traced it with her fingertip, her face softened, the doomed accorded the tenderness that was their due. Young men dying in their prime. He put his hand on top of hers. This is what the place called for. Halting, inarticulate encounters. Trysts in the dark. He put his arms around her. The kiss felt awkward. They knew it needed to be this way, fumbled at, snatched, fearful of discovery, the usher's torch turned on you.

'And this,' she said.

GABRIEL, ELSPETH BET A $ V A X

'What does it mean?'
'X stands for a kiss.'
'Bet a dollar to a kiss.'
'Gabriel.'

'The same man?'

'Yes.'

'The soldier and his girl, Gabriel and Elspeth.' The cinema for a moment full of lost lovers, soft presences.

'He was telling the truth,' Cole said.

'I came here in the night. I found it.'

'They used to sit up here as well.'

'Who did?'

'Harper and Reay. In the same seat.'

'They brought you?'

'They brought me once.'

'What was the film?'

'The Way We Were'. They made me sit in the stalls. Tell them if the usher was coming.'

'They were safe with you.'

'No.'

'Why?'

'She broke a vase of lilies.'

'What?'

'After Harper left.'

'Tell me.'

The Matron had left a vase of lilies on the table in the hallway of the home. Cole saw it broken on the sprung pine floor, the lilies white against the polished wood, shards of porcelain and water spilled across the boards. It was like a country house mystery. There would be whispers in the sculleries, scuttling feet on the back stairs. *Reay did it.*

'Upritchard came up from the boiler room. He sent me to the graveyard on the river bank.'

'For what?'

'For sally rods. Willow branches.'

Harper had told him about the workhouse funerals. The procession to the waste ground by the river. The bottom of the coffin was bracketed with brass hinges screwed to the baseplate so that it could be reused. Other inmates filled in the grave. The corpses stripped naked so that the clothes could be reused. All surrendered before they entered the workhouse. They died of typhoid, pneumonia, tuberculosis. What prayers the dead got were lost in the boreal darkness. Cole gathering the rods, stripping leaves from them.

'What did he want them for?'

'I never asked. I brought them back up and gave them to him. He told me to go.'

'What did he want them for?'

Cole could hear a girl's voice. He went to the door that opened onto the boiler room stairs. The stairs were dusty, rough-cut planks, insulation and pipework at head height. Later he would learn the meaning of these rooms, window-less, utilitarian, beyond the reach of mercy. Reay's back was white between the welts, Lynch pinning her hands in front of her, Upritchard standing over the girl, his sleeves rolled up, a man at labour, the rod in his hand stripped of bark. A hand on his shoulder pulled Cole away from the door.

'You should have helped her.'

'There was nothing I could do.'

'Who pulled you away?'

'Corry.'

'He asked me not to,' Kay said.

'Who?'

'Corry.'

'I don't want to know.'

'I made a deal.'

'Don't tell me. He fell. It was an accident.'

'I tossed him for it. Live or die.' She took something from her pocket. A silver coin. She flicked it, spinning in the dark, looking as if it would never come down.

'He lost. Your turn.'

'Turn for what?'

'To tell the truth. Reay said they wrote their names on the seats but I couldn't find them.'

'How did you know about that, about them writing their names?'

'It was in the letters.'

'Who gave you the letters?'

'The Matron gave me my mother's letters. She said they belonged to me.' She looked him in the eyes. *Tell me what you did. Tell me you didn't post the letters. We are beleaguered by our own selves sometimes, and are therefore helpless. Tell me something less than the truth, I won't demand more, my heart won't hold you to it.*

He said nothing. He watched her walk away from him down the balcony steps. He heard the auditorium door open and bang shut. Girls' names adrift in his memory. The town at dusk, walls blackened in the salt wind. Girls walking off into the night afterwards, heads together, the whispered tellings. Elspeth. Reay. Kay. Waiting for the backward glance. Waiting for them to look back just once.

*

Letter #4

Fingers and toes fingers and toes that's what mothers do to new babies count the fingers and toes.

I waited and waited for you to come for us my love. The film was The Way We Were with Barbra Streisand and Robert Redford they were young and only had eyes for each other you said you be Barbra and I'll be Robert.

There were achy songs and an empty seat beside me do you remember the night we writ our names along with all the others the soldiers and sailors and lovers of all the years you says who knows what's on these seats Barbra and Robert sing Evergreen to each other on the screen it's the place people come to love in the dark over all these years is that what happiness is just kissing in the dark felt like it to me.

You promised us you never came lover.

I decided the girl baby's name call her Kay.

They're after me Lynch and Upritchard and Corry they call themselves the Brethren the Matron told me the bloodhounds are out howling across the bayou do bloodhounds howl or do they bay it doesn't matter now my own bloodhounds are calling me.

You remember me and you and Ghost out on the sand dunes and I hid on youse behind the hut we were laughing and you were both looking for me all the time I was laughing and saying you can't see me you can't see me.

Twenty-six

Morne Ferry Terminal
1st December 2000

Cole is standing on the wall of the swimming pool behind the dive team searching for the body. He looks at the monitor, the feed coming from the lead diver's camera. The seafloor is lit by halogen light. A few metres down. Exhaled nitrogen in the top left-hand corner. Disturbed sediment floats across the lens. Visibility at one or two metres. Always something sinister about these shots, the seafloor murk, the greyscale, debris borne by the current. The diver's gloved hand is sometimes visible in front of the lens. The shape of a boat appears in frame, sunk in the silt, intact though some of the planks are sprung. The mast has fallen across the foredeck, hanks of weed hang from the rigging and bent rails. Something moves at the edge of the frame, a wreckfish or moray disturbed by the light. Gone down into the deep companionways, the fish holds, the lightless ballast. The boat is canted to one side and the camera moves along the hull. Looking for something. There can be no other reason for this scrutiny of the half-rotted planking, the paint lifted in blisters, tiny limpets and horse barnacles in gaps between the planks.

The diver's gloves and watch are in shot now. Dive time is limited. The fish-hold hatch is visible. The diver moves across the deck, through the debris, the steel core cable from the winch housing tangled in the otter boards, the broken rails, jagged mast tines, crossing dangerous terrain, there's a risk of getting snagged, ruptured air hoses. The camera yaws and the monitor screen shows rusted stanchions, broken deck plating. A man could die down here, trapped in the debris. It pays to be careful. The camera steadies. Granular matter fills the screen as the hatch cover is pulled off. Then it settles.

The water in the fish hold is clear. The bottom of the hold is foot-deep in sediment and sand. A shore crab backs away from the camera. The halogen light is contained in the narrow space so that visibility is good. The body comes into focus. Its eye sockets are very dark. They stand out in the burning white light. John Lynch seems to be looking at the camera through small fleshless orbs, the obsidian lens of the night.

It is late evening, darkness long fallen. The last cars have come off the ferry. It is sailing. Several container lorries gleaming with rain parked on the ferry apron, their everydayness fading with the light, gathering sinister intent to themselves. Where were the others of the town? Had the town taken them, consumed them in the great sin of itself? Were the canals being dragged for corpses, open spaces combed? You felt the emptiness of the rest of the harbour area, the unpeopled void. A camera on its gantry feeding back to a room somewhere, a watcher.

Kay stood on the deck of the ferry. She can see Cole in the distance standing on the edge of the swimming pool. If he looked up he might see her, but he doesn't. He's wearing a raincoat and carries a leather briefcase under his arm. He looks wearied, burdened. You get lost in your past. You get marooned by your lies.

She felt the deck plates flex beneath her feet as the ship gathered way, sitting low in the water, the sea barely stirring at the forefoot. Drivers did not stay in the cabs during crossings. The trucks shifted on their beds and the bulkheads creaked and moaned. There were shadows on the salt-corroded gangways. Kay thought it like a submerged hulk, the domain of drowned mariners. She could find the dead wherever she went. They were waiting for her.

She sees the harbour lights on either side. The cold and the rain. The reflection of the Haulbowline light on the underside of low cloud, the carbide glow. The factory ships out beyond the bar. Slabs of frozen herring are thawing on the concrete trawler pier. The pier light on. The channel markers. The Lee Stone. The Mew Island. Haulbowline. Points of light in the darkness.

Looking up to the wheelhouse Kay can see the pilot's face underlit by the Decca screen. There was little sea traffic. A freighter riding at anchor outside the bar. The pilot boat on an easterly heading, static and chatter on the marine band over her head coming from the open wheelhouse window. The ferry cleared the pierhead and changed heading, feeling the heft of the swell as it took up slack and the ship's bows turned towards a new bearing, the VHF fading out. The crackles. The wavering sound levels. The sound of a last transmission. Fading off into wow and flutter, the needles hitting their end stops. Drowned out in the cosmic static.

Kay looked beyond the Haulbowline light to the caravan park on the aerodrome hardstandings close to the sea. Overgrown silos and bomb shelters. The shadowed expanse. The airbase concrete leading down to the tideline. Isolated concrete structures. Hangar buildings with asbestos roofs. The doors and windows were blocked with rusted sheet tin. At night nothing moved on the empty aprons and runways. The infantry units had embarked for dispersal points in England over several days, then embarked onto ships for the Omaha Beach landings, nineteen and twenty years old, machine-gunned in the shallows, dragged under by their pack, their remains scattered on the beachheads.

The place had an out-of-season feel to it even in the summer. The aluminium caravan cladding scoured by sand, blown across from the hardstandings. Women set out picnic tables beside the caravans, worn and sun-faded deckchairs. It was what they took from the world. Cautious and thrifty, working towards small pleasures that had to be earned, something to set against the lough and its dusk sea fogs and the east wind that moaned at night. The still tower of the Bomb Loft visible above the caravan roofs. This is when the grace of the town lingers, winter evenings, rain on the streets, lights coming on early along the Esplanade. The pavements are empty, the car parks deserted. On the height above the town the empty windows of the hospital, the exterior render fallen away in places to show the stone outline underneath of the workhouse it had once been. She thought of coffins brought in a handcart down a sunken pathway after dark. The grave opened by lamplight. A pauper's moon hidden by the scrub pines growing on the slope. The collapsed chinoiserie of the swimming pool slipping past, the ship's wash on the decks of the grounded trawler. In the distance the empty pleasure grounds of Sugar Island, the roofs and shivering glass doors of the cinema, the Vogue, the place where promises are made and not kept. The screen held still in the moment before something happens, the silvered dusk of the century.